MAC 2007

Sgt. Vlengles' Revenge

And Other Abuses of Power

To Richard –
Woof !

Thanks for Reading

Tim ___

SGT. VLENGLES' REVENGE

AND OTHER ABUSES OF POWER

By TIM BROUGH

A Boner Book by,
The Nazca Plains Corporation
Las Vegas, NV
2003

ISBN: 1-887-895-51-5

Published by,   The Nazca Plains Corporation ®
                        4640 Paradise Rd, Suite 141
                        Las Vegas NV 89109-8000

PUBLISHER'S NOTE:

This is a work of fiction. Names, characters, places, and incidents either are the products of the author's imagination or are used fictitiously, and any resemblance to actual persons, living or dead, business establishments, events or locales is entirely coincidental.

Editor, Ty Evans

Photographer, Robert Bishop

Cover Models, Jayden

Author, Tim Brough

DEDICATION

Before I owned my first leather jacket, I put out explorative contacts to men that looked like they may be safe havens for my inexperience. One of those tendrils was to a writer of a column in The Leather Journal, "Rope Rap." When I finally screwed up enough courage to leave for Los Angeles, he told me that I was welcome to visit him and his partner. He was the first leather person I'd ever met.

Thus began what I can only describe as one of the strongest and most satisfying friendships of my life. Paul "Papa Bear" Sehm took me to my first leather bar (Griff's) and introduced me to many wonderful people in the L.A. leather community, including my first Master. I once joked that I'd spent more weekends in his bed than most of his play partners without ever once going beyond platonic. Yet he never made me ever feel less loved or nurtured because of that, and if there were to be any one man I would call my Mentor, it would be him.

It saddens me that we lost Paul to cancer in 1994, before any of my first kink stories were published. This collection of stories is dedicated to his memory. As an avid reader of anything he could get his hands on and a lover of only the finest smut, "Papa Bear" would have loved every page.

ACKNOWLEDGMENTS

It's only been a few months since I wrote the first set of acknowledgments for "Black Gloves, White Magic." So the list here will be short and sweet. I have to thank all the folks who stepped up to the plate for round one.

Masters Alex Keppeler and Steve Sampson, for making me look good.

Rich W, Rich G, Rich R, Eric, Ray, Scott, Thom and Jay and everyone at TLA Entertainment.

Matthew and Alan for being the first two to put money in my hand for their copies. Lambda Rising in Washington, DC, Michael and Richard at Leather Masters II in Allentown, Jim Madden at the Bike Stop in Philly, and Daddy Bob and Kim at Black Hawk leather in Houston, for the first meet the author signings.

Sir Alan and the staff of Station House Leathers for making IML and Folsom Street East happen in such an amazing way.

Larry Townsend for the wonderful compliments and taking BG/WM on for your flyers.

Also Ken Barnes, Master Dennis, slave Patrick, Sir Doug, Dave Rhodes, Robert Steele, Jayden, Ty Evans, Master Thomas, Master Gerry, PGN, and anyone who took on inventory.

My family, for not freaking out when they heard exactly what the first book was.

And of course, Papa Joel.

FOWARD

When a good friend asks you to write the foreword to his second book, you're often at a loss as to what might be best written or what might be best left unsaid. Such is the case between Tim and me.

I met Tim some ten years ago when he came to Chicago as a slave applicant. The weekend didn't go quite like his story "To Explode In Beauty," but we did begin what has become a fine and enduring friendship. During those years, I've seen Tim move to California and to the Southwest desert and back to California and then to Pennsylvania. I've watched him struggle with his publications, his relationships, and his life.

During those years his writing, as you can see herein, has been fine-tuned to a horny edge. Even if these stories are fiction, I can see the real Tim behind his characters. The nice thing about fiction, of course, is that it doesn't have to be real, though Tim knows his craft well enough to make it realistic.

Yes, he is a pushy bottom and an author, which means too, that he probably wants ME to help inspire another story when I ask him to autograph this collection. It will be my pleasure to do so, since I also notice that he has some gall to debunk those seven myths about Masters and Tops. I'll have to remember that the next time we're in a dungeon together, with Tim's Daddy Joel's permission, of course.

So that leaves me wondering who is Doctor Terror and what fire station did Tim mess around in?

Like I wrote above, some things are best left unsaid. I can, though, agree with Butch God who says "I know a bargain when I see one." This book is adeal. Enough of me, now read on and enjoy.

Jack Rinella
Chicago, IL

CONTENTS

Sgt. Vlengles' Revenge

And Other Abuses of Power

SGT. VLENGLES REVENGE'

The lake was still shimmering in the pre-sundown light. The birds who made their nests in the trees along the shore were already flying for home, their day of food gathering complete. As for two men in their rowboat, they were still waiting for one last catch. Or, at least, one of them was.

"Come on man. We've already got three bass in the boat. Let's get to shore before dark." The man speaking was a hefty lumberjack of a man and he had the beard to show it. He was staring anxiously at the smaller man on the other side of the boat; a shorter but clean shaven man named Dar.

Dar kicked away the empty beer cans that had piled around his boots from a day's time on the water. "Yeah, alright already. Besides, I don't want any more fish. I really want one boy bitch!" Dar laughed, then belched loud enough to send an echo across the waters. The man across from him sighed below his beard, and Dar could see it. "What's the matter, Terry? You're not turning wuss on me, are you?"

Terry stared down at the beer cans surrounding Dar's boots. "Hey, fucking some redneck tied in the woods is fine. But why did you have to burn his car?"

"Because that is why we'll never get caught," Dar said with a smirk. "I told him, right before I threw my cigarette through the window with the gas, that if I thought for a moment he'd squeal, he'd have been in the trunk." Dar laughed again. "You saw him! He all but shit himself! Then he ran so fast a rabbit wouldn't have caught him."

Terry took up the oars and started steering the boat towards shore. "Sure Dar, sure. I also remember being scared as hell that you were going to fry the kid. I know that you're edgy, but that was way over the top." The dock lamps came into view as he rowed in closer. "If we spot some hustler freak on the way home, I'm not saying we don't take him. But damn! Keep it under control, man!"

Ripples were lapping against the dock. Dar stood to his full six feet and threw the line to the waiting attendant. "Stop being such a nell, Terr. We find one, we play with one. The car thing was just one deal, okay?"

Terry didn't respond. He just handed the day's catch up to the dock for preparation. The camp kitchen would skin and de-bone it, then deliver it to their campsite tomorrow morning, for a pan fry dinner later.

"Let's take a ride before getting back," Dar decided. "I love riding through the woods after dark. You can never be sure of what may jump out." He looked over at Terry and raised his hands like bear claws above his head. "Rowrrrr!" he bellowed, and set to laughing again. Terry just picked up his leather jacket and walked off towards their bikes.

Dar's jacket was still draped over his bike, an old Yamaha Police Cruiser from his days of being director of operations at the State Police Training Academy. He had loved that job, and it fulfilled two of his grandest dreams. He was finally making a good salary in a Law Enforcement profession, and every year a whole new class of young men obeyed his every word and called him SIR at the beginning and end of each spoken sentence. There had always been rumors about why some of his favored cadets landed in fast track jobs straight after graduation, and horror stories of bloodied riding crops and cadets secretly bullwhipped for their disobedience.

It was exactly one of those rumors that took him into early retirement, when a first year cadet named Jackson accused Dar of caning him for his attitude and lack of respect towards training. He also had bright red streaks across his ass as proof. Despite the rumors and stories that had circulated before, hundreds of former students of Sgt. Dar Vlengles came forward with letters of praise, recommendation, and in-person character reports. But the damage had already been done. Jackson's case was dismissed and he was expelled, Sgt. Dar Vlengles was given the option to take an early retirement before a second investigation would take place. The State Police had a great deal of respect for their headmaster, and the offer was more than generous. Sgt. Vlengles took the offer and retired to his new home in the Poconos for, as he claimed, "peace, quiet, fishing, and raising hell on his motorcycle."

Dar did have one secret he didn't share. Most of the stories, while exaggerated into legendary proportion, were true. Jackson had been caned. He had also been a willing and eager cock sucker, but when Dar refused to change a midterm grade in his favor, Jackson decided to get revenge. Dar knew better than to admit to the act, and since Jackson's public attitude towards his superiors was well known, a published report by several cadets stating Jackson had said he was working on a plan to "Fuck over Sarge for good" was brought up in the trial proceedings. Once that fact had been introduced, it was easy to hang Jackson as a vindictive punk with no right to become a state police officer. Jackson disappeared and Dar's name was cleared. Dar packed his secret toy locker and found new friends to play with.

Terry came into his retirement as a chiropractor to the stars. In his prime, his New York office client list read like a Broadway Agent's talent roster. Terry delivered excellence to those willing to pay for it, and Terry also took no small delight that many of these leading men would scream out in agony as he adjusted their spines. That led to a slightly more interesting position when he joined a bondage club and discovered that a lot of men had a thing for Master Doctors. He discovered that many men were willing to pay a large amount of cash to be roughly examined and ordered about by a man in a white coat.

Fate dealt him a slightly different hand when a car accident left him with a compound fracture in both legs and a broken jaw. Even after surgery, the scars remained on his face, and the legs couldn't handle the pressure of a full day of seeing patients. He retired, sold his apartment in New York City, and set up business in his Pocono ranch home. That business had a client roster more into the adjustments that his bondage club slave boys desired, and Doctor Terry Sir was comfortable with his second source of income. He bought himself a new Honda Gold Wing and, ironically enough, had been given the nickname Doctor Terror by his neighbors after he grew a beard to cover the scars on his jaw. It seemed that a large bearded leather wearing man on a motorcycle amused Terry's neighbors and gave Terry the chance to play up his image as a local teddy bear biker rather than the images they didn't know of in the attic office.

It was by coincidence that Terry met Dar. There had been a lot of talk about the Davis house being bought by this former police academy superintendent, but Terry wasn't one to join in the rumor mill. It took a few weeks, but Terry was pulling into Foodland just as Dar was coming out with his groceries. Dar stopped to admire the Honda and asked how long Terry had been a rider. Terry replied "I bought a motor scooter at 17, and I've had something with two wheels and an engine ever since."

Dar smiled and pointed over at his police cruiser. "That's mine. I bought it from the force at my retirement and I've been riding something like that for at least 20 years now." He extended his hand to Terry and introduced himself. "Dar Vlengles, retired state police. And you are?"

"Dr. Terry Miller, retired spinal cracker." He laughed at the expression on Dar's face, until Dar replied.

"You're the legendary Dr. Terror? These little old blue hairs have a lot of stories about you!" Dar laughed again, "And I'm sure that all of them are true." Terry felt the red of embarrassment working up his neck, but Dar continued. "I know you're retired and all, but could I ask for a treatment? I pulled my shoulder riding the other night and I'm willing to pay for it. What do you say?"

Terry had to think. The only back working he had done for almost five years was from men chained to tables with other medical instruments in positions not intended with original use. But Dar was turning on both all the charm he'd learned as a public figure and all the unspoken presence of command that was his driving personality force. Terry fished into his pocket and gave a business card to Dar, and agreed to a visit that evening.

When Dar arrived early, Terry had not completely cleaned the study where he had placed a folding worktable to adjust Dar. But he welcomed Dar into the room and instructed him to remove as much clothing as he felt comfortable with. Dar's response was to strip naked. While Terry was a little surprised, he was gratified to see a beautiful ass climb atop his table and stretch out. He wondered to himself how his riding crop would sound against something so tight. He knew he couldn't be thinking of that kind of session right then, so he concentrated on the shoulders of the man lying before him.

The pressure felt great to Dar, and he moaned in response. He opened his eyes and glanced at the desk by the table. His skin automatically tightened when he noticed a barely visible link to a set of handcuffs. Terry noticed the tension and asked if he had come across a particularly sore point.

"Oh, not that, Doctor. It was just those handcuffs under the desk there. You tried to hide them, and if it weren't for my old cop instincts, I wouldn't have spotted them. So tell me, what's a mild mannered country doc like you doing with restraints?"

Terry was at a loss. "What do you think I do with them?"

Dar gave Terry every particle of bad cop eye contact he could, and replied, "I think some of your patients might be turning the tables on you. Isn't that true? Doctor Terror?"

Something clicked in Terry's mind. "Mr. Vlengles, if you are going to come into my office with that attitude, I suggest you get on the floor and on your knees. Then I will show you what I am doing with handcuffs. And you will address me as Doctor Sir. "

Dar exploded with laughter. "Doctor Sir? I love it! I have never called anyone Sir unless they had more stars or bars than me!" He sat up on the edge of the table. "Let me guess. You have a steady flow of clients willing to call you Doctor Sir? I'll tell you that I had plenty of cadets calling me Sir, and more than a few of them tasted handcuffs and bullwhips. It seems we have more in common than motorcycles, don't we, Doc?"

The barrier broken, both men described their histories and favorite pastimes. Before the night was over, they decided to form a sort of working relationship. If one Master had a slave in need of what the other had to offer, they would set up a meeting. If they found a slave who wanted the combined expertise of two Masters, they would invite the other Master over for the session. For the next three years, they expanded on this relationship, learning techniques from each other and inventing new methods as they went along. The little blue haired ladies still called Terry "Doctor Terror," but they also added a new friend to their list. A man with a funny looking last name that they all started calling "Sarge."

That relationship remained strong till a few weeks before this fishing trip. Terry was getting used to his friend's taste for beer, and for his heavy play with men who wanted to be interrogated by the meanest cop they could find. That night, while on a ride through the woods, they spotted an obvious cruiser leaning against the trunk of his car. They pulled up beside him and asked if he needed any help or if he was looking for something. The guy replied, "I'm looking for some rocks to get off."

Dar grabbed him by the collar and said, "What if we just decided to make you?"

A flicker of fear crossed the man's eyes and he murmured "Anything you say Sir."

Terry dug into his jacket pocket on produced a quarter. "Who goes first, Sarge? I think I want those pouting lips around my nuts." Terry spun the quarter in the air as Sarge kept staring into the face of tonight's obvious toy. "Well, wouldn't that be a shame, because I was just wondering what he would say with my dick up his ass." He didn't let his eyes lose contact for even a blink Staring into the eyes of the man he was holding off the ground, Dar continued. "What do you say, Doc? Heads I win, tails you lose?"

Terry's quarter spun into the air and was snatched on its way down. Opening his palm, he mocked a sigh. "Damn, tails." He looked at the man in the air and whispered, "You lose!"

At the signal, Dar threw the man to the ground and Terry slapped a pair of handcuffs across his wrists. Dar was already ripping the jeans away for the slave's legs, while pulling his own fly down. Terry was shoving his gloved thumb deep into the man's mouth, warning him to loosen up for what was coming next.

"And you better do what Doc tells you to. He gets really pissed off when slaves don't obey." Dar growled from behind. The two Masters pushed the slave into the trees and bent him over a low hanging branch. Terry pulled a piece of rope from his vest and fastened the slave over the limb, leaving both his ass and mouth available. Dar pulled his belt out from his pants and began warming up the slave for his fuck, while Terry stood in front and slapped the slave's face with his erection.

It wasn't long before both Masters were riding their slave in a see saw rhythm as Terry took the front and Dar rode the back. The slave had said he wanted to get some rocks off, and the blow job he was giving Terry made him know he had guessed right. But it was obvious that having Dar inside him was not what the slave had bargained for, and he was bucking and squirming to try to make this slave-rape end. Of course, this struggle just made Dar all the more willing to prolong the agony, even as Terry was getting close to losing his load. The explosion was enough to make Terry shudder and roar into the night, as Dar continued bucking the slave's ass. After he caught his breath, Terry looked and Dar and asked, "How's he riding, Sarge?"

"Pretty good so far, Doc. But he isn't bleeding and he isn't crying. You think he's going to cry for me?"

The slave bucked, cursed, and raised his head above the log. "Hey fuckers! When I get out of this, I will make you pay. You hear that Sarge? I'll take you down, you bastard!"

That was when Terry saw something in Sarge he'd never seen before. Pure, untethered rage. Dar ripped the restraining rope from the branch and, still firmly rooted in the slave's ass, lifted him into a standing position while he threw a choke hold around the man's neck.

The slave began gasping in shock as Dar squeezed his arm tighter against his windpipe. "Nobody takes me down! You understand that? Nobody! You want to die, asshole? You're about one minute away from having the last cum load you'll ever feel! Well? You want to die now?"

Terry ran over and tried to pull Dar's arm from around the slave's neck, but Dar was too strong, and too angry. He kept squeezing the slave's neck tighter and slamming at his ass. Panic was coming into the slave's face as he struggled to get air, but Dar suddenly screamed as he pumped his load and the slave's insides felt the pulsing force of a huge ejaculation fighting to find room. Dar let off on the choke and the slave fell to the ground, gasping for breath. He was so terrified that within seconds, he was throwing up onto the forest floor.

"What the hell was that?" Terry ran over to Dar and pushed him away from the slave's heaving body. "What the hell brought that on?"

Dar just looked at Terry and sneered. "Best mind fuck I think I have ever delivered, right Doctor? There's still more to come." Dar broke away from Terry and lifted the slave by the handcuffs. The slave screamed in pain, spittle and vomit spraying from his face, as Dar drug him towards the road. Dar groped into the slave's pockets until he found the keys, and then he found the one that opened the trunk. "Well, well, what have we here? Spare gas in the trunk? That's very illegal, boy. Did you know that? It's also very, very dangerous. Let me show you."

Dar took a cigarette from his jacket and lit it. "Just a tiny little spark from carpet static could set it off," he told the slave. Taking an arcing swing with the can, he smashed the passenger side car window and threw the open can inside. The smell of pouring fuel rushed out the open window as tension outside the car increased. "I told you slave, no one will ever take me down. If I even thought for a minute that you might come back and try." Dar lowered his voice to the slave's ear and whispered something Terry couldn't hear. But Terry did see how ashen the slave's face had been after puking his guts out pale even whiter. Dar laughed a sickeningly evil laugh and flicked his cigarette into the car. An immediate whoosh of fire engulfed the interior as the slave began to struggle and scream at the sight of his car going up in smoke. Dar continued laughing as he dropped the slave to the roadside. Terry took that as his opportunity to un-cuff the slave and quickly pulled him back up to his feet. The slave took one last look at Dar, and ran as fast as he could.

"That's right, you little punk! Run away, and hope Sarge never finds you again!" He continued with the hysterical laughing until Terry grabbed him by his jacket sleeve, and jerked him towards where their bikes were parked. Mounting his Goldwing, Terry shouted to Dar. "Damn it, you got to lay off the damn beer!" He revved his bike and burned rubber away from the flaming pile that used to look like an automobile. Dar was quick to follow.

That was three weeks ago. Terry had not seen the angry look on Dar's face since that night and he ultimately figured it was due to the beer. There had been a couple other dual play sessions, and they had all come off without a hitch. As luck would have this particular evening, they were only a few minutes ride away from the fishing dock when they spotted a car pulled off to the side. Its trunk was open and a frustrated looking man was kicking a flat tire. Terry and Dar coasted up to the vehicle and asked the man if he was in any trouble. Dar was already feeling like this was a potential score. The man kicked at his tire again. "No, but thanks. Just a damned flat. Damn back roads." He looked up at the two bikers idling next to him. They looked safe enough, so he asked "Do you think you could help me with the jack?"

"Sure," Dar replied. He went around behind the car and took a look in the trunk. The jack was there, all right. So was a leather satchel with a K.J. monogram. It was already partly opened, so Dar took a look inside. He kept his mouth shut and his face blank, but he saw wrist and ankle restraints, a riding crop, and at least one piece of rope. "Damn," he thought, "he's a top!"

Grabbing the jack, Dar came around the front of the vehicle, where Terry and the driver were already prying the hubcap off the bad tire. "Hey Doc, why don't you get the spare out of the trunk?" When Terry cast a questioning glance back to Dar, Dar cocked his head in the direction of the trunk and put a lock like grip around his wrist. Terry knew that Dar had discovered something, and got up off the gravel.

"Okay Sarge. I'll get it." If Dar was speaking in code names, that meant he was looking at this as a real potential playmate. When he got a look at the satchel in the trunk, he thought the same thing. Terry hoisted the spare from the trunk well and rolled it to the front of the car, where Dar and the driver were fitting the jack into place. "Nice bag you got back there. I got one just like it in my Doctor's office."

Without looking up, the driver began turning the jack crank to raise the car. "Really now," he said with little expression.

Terry moved over the man on the ground, and Dar planted his feet across from the driver. "Yes, I do," Terry answered. "The real amazing thing is, we seem to carry the same equipment.

The driver looked up at the leather bikers and shot a contemptuous glance to both of them. "Yes, but I get paid for it. Who'd pay a pair of old geezers like you to collar them?"

"How much?" Dar's eyes narrowed down to narrow slits. "Who'd let an arrogant S.O.B. like you put a collar on them?"

Terry saw the glower on Dar's face and decided to cut this episode short. "Hey. Buddy, we stopped to offer you help. If you don't want it, we're out of here." He put his hand on Dar's shoulder and tried to nudge him away.

The driver let a sneering look pass between him and Dar, and said "Five Hundred, plus fifty more for any penetration or cum shots. Of course for you, I may do a charity fuck. Now why don't you old boys hit the road and let a real Master get the work done."

Dar threw Terry's hand off his shoulder and produced his wallet. He flipped it open and shoved it into the driver's stunned face. "I don't know your name, but you are under arrest for solicitation of a police officer. Cuff him, Doc."

Terry was laughing so hard that, even with his misgivings, he took his cuffs out and slapped them on the wrists of the driver. If anyone needed a lesson in manners, it was this guy. Dar was reading him his rights and patting him down. He produced the driver's wallet and started flipping through the cards. When the drivers' license came up, Dar tossed the wallet to the ground and read off the name on the license. Then his eyes went very dark. "Doc," he said to Terry without taking his eyes off the card in his hand, "We have a special treat in store for us tonight. Get him in the trunk."

Terry maneuvered the prisoner towards the rear of his own car and shoved him inside. Dar pulled a strip of duct tape from a roll that was inside the trunk, and after stuffing a rag in the mouth of their suspect, taped it into place. The trunk lid was slammed down and the only sound to be heard was the muffled cries from under the metal. Dar picked up the spare and threw it into the back seat of the car before he and Terry mounted their bikes.

"I'll come back for him after we drop off the bikes at my place. But take a look at the license and just remember that name. I've got one hell of a story to tell you."

His police cruiser spit gravel as he charged down the road, and Terry was close behind.

When they returned to the house, Dar looked at Terry and asked, "Do you remember the name on the license?"

Terry looked over from where he was tarping his bike. "Kevin Jackson, right?"

"Damn right," Dar shot back. "Remember how I told you that a student who was trying to accuse me of torturing him? He's about two miles away in a car trunk right now. I'm going to drive down and fetch him from his car and see just how fondly he remembers his old friend Sgt. Vlengles." He looked up at the old certifications above the fireplace and took a deep breath. "I've been waiting for this day a long time. Doc, go make sure the discipline room is well prepared, and keep the fireplace going. I'll be right back." Terry heard him laughing as he went out to his truck, and he braced for the worst.

It wasn't long before Terry heard the sound of Dar's pickup pulling up in the driveway behind the house, and he could see Dar pulling a man with a pillowcased head out of the truck bed. The man was covered in dirt and mud, but Terry didn't recall any landfill in the back of Dar's truck.

"Poor boy didn't want to come out of the trunk quietly, Doc," Dar said as he pushed the prisoner in through the kitchen door. "Mr. Jackson, Mr. Kevin Jackson. Have a seat." Dar pushed Jackson into a kitchen chair and gave a nod to Terry. Chains and locks were used to immobilize their prisoner. Dar continued his monologue, the one he'd been rehearsing in his mind for over twelve years. "The man with the chains is my good friend Doc. My good friends call me Sarge. Some older acquaintances call me Sergeant. We're going to take you into the living room for a little fireside chat."

Terry grabbed hold of the chair and wheeled Jackson over by the hearth. Dar put his hand on the top of the pillowcase and continued. "Mr. Jackson, we are going to have a game of word and phrase association. I will give you a word or phrase and you will tell me the first thing that pops into your tiny brain." The pillowcase came away with a whip, and the gag still taped over Jackson's mouth was ripped away hard. As Jackson was attempting to spit the rag out from his mouth, Dar took a seat across from him. "Let's begin. The first word will be Sergeant."

Jackson finally managed to throw the rag to the floor and coughed out "Asshole."

Dar looked over at Terry and Terry sent one hard glove covered backhand across Jackson's face. "Wrong answer, Jackson. Now why don't we be a good little student and not make Doc have to bash you in the face again, shall we? Next word. Cadet."

"Old Queens." Jackson blew a wad of spit towards Dar. Terry reacted with a double backhand, first right, then left. The blows cracked Jackson's lip. "Bad, bad, little cadet." Dar mocked. "I'll warn you this once. The next hit comes with a closed fist. Now, let's try a time association. Eighteen years ago." Jackson sat silent. "Too hard for you, cadet? Let's put them all in a row for you then. Sergeant. Cadet. Eighteen years ago."

The sudden change in Jackson's expression gave him away. He knew whom he was sitting across from, and it scared the hell out of him. He looked into Dar's eyes and recognized the fierce determined expression that told him he either earns the grades, or he goes home. His mouth went dry and his balls shriveled into his crotch.

"One more try, Cadet Jackson. Fill in the blank. Sergeant."

Jackson spit the blood off his lip and replied, "Vlengles, Sir."

Terry looked to Dar and saw the immediate satisfaction of a man who just broke his most challenging slave. Deciding that this session just might be as special as Dar was anticipating, he lifted the fireplace poker from the hot ashes and put its smoking point just centimeters from Jackson's face. "So tell me then, Cadet Jackson. What should we do to student slave punks that turn on their mentors?"

Jackson could only stare at the poker waving back and forth before his eyes. "I don't know, Sir. Can you please forgive me, Sirs?" The rattle of the chains matched Jackson's quivers. Doc put the poker back down.

It was a sound that pleased Dar like no other. "There is no forgiveness for you, Cadet Jackson. As you recall, I was publicly humiliated before the entire state, and forced to quit a job I'd loved for almost twenty years, and knew exactly why the lashes were on your ass. In the boiler room of bunker 27, you begged the Sergeant to hurt you till you could take it like a man. You got exactly what you wished for, tied over a sawhorse with a horse bridal in your teeth. You walked out of there with your ass turned to grass and a smile on your face. You wanted a caning so bad that those slash marks you showed to the Commander were already a week old. And all because you got a C on your regulations exam. You told me you were going to take me down, Cadet." Dar made a sweeping motion around the room they were in. "Tell me, does this look like brought down to you?"

15

Terry put his hands on the back of the chair, tilting it off the floor. "From here on out, you address me as Doctor Sir, and him as Sgt. Sir. Are you clear about that?"

Jackson's face and forehead had gone wet with sweat. "Yes Sir, Doctor Sir and Sgt. Sir." Dar picked up the front legs of the chair and lifted Jackson off the ground.

As they began heading for a basement door, Dar told Jackson, "I have been waiting eighteen years wondering if I'd ever see you again. Damn son, you need to take better care of your tires." As they began carting Jackson down the steps, Dar told him "This is a special part of my house. Some of the furniture may not look familiar to you, but we're going to re-associate you with some of your first loves." Dar and Terry set the chair down next to Dar's stocks. As Terry was unlocking the chains, Dar was separating the boards that he was preparing to confine Cadet Jackson in. "Tell me, Cadet. When did you turn top on us?"

Jackson was still looking for a way to delay the punishment and maybe escape. But the chains were not all removed, so he decided to try and appease Sgt. Vlengles. "After I was expelled, Sir, I met a trucker from Pittsburgh. He told me to spank him for being such a poor father to his sonny boy. He was also ready to give me fifty bucks for it. I just remembered how you worked on me and gave it back. As soon as I found out that people would give me money for beating ass, I just started putting classifieds in sex papers and waited for the phone calls, Sir."

Terry was removing the last of the chain from Cadet Jackson's wrists. "What did you like the most about this, Cadet?"

Jackson stood at attention in front of Sgt. Vlengles and answered "The money, Doctor Sir."

Terry looked up with a stare. "The money? What else, Cadet?"

Cadet Jackson looked quizzically at Terry. "I don't know, Doctor Sir." He felt a sudden jerk from behind as Dar pulled him by the back of his collar.

Dar snorted in ridicule. "You're as dumbass a top as you were a cadet, Jackson. It must be time to teach you some of the basics." Forcing Jackson's head in between the slats, Dar closed them over Jackson's neck and wrists. Fastening the lock on the stock's peg latch, Dar motioned, "This is control, and I control you. Making you helpless turns me on. Knowing you're scared turns me on. Knowing I will make you feel terror really turns me on." He went around to the back of the stocks and slapped Jackson's ass. "Doc, how do you think we should get his pants down? Just pull them off?"

Terry put his hands on Jackson's face and forced a bearded sloppy kiss down his mouth. Pulling himself up, he laughed and replied "That's far too easy on the boy, Sarge. How about using this?" Reaching to the tool rack along the wall, Terry brought down a box cutter. He moved behind the stocks to where Dar stood and began cutting Jackson's jeans off in ribbon strips. When the ribbons were all that was left hanging around the slave's waist, Terry tore the remaining fabric off with his gloved hands.

"Hell, the kid wears boxers," Dar laughed. "Give me that blade, Doc." As Dar began sawing through the elastic waistband, he commented, "Remember what I said about control, Cadet? Tell me how you feel right now."

Cadet Jackson took a mule kick at his two captors, but missed. "I'll hammer your brains in if you even fucking nick me with that thing!"

Sarge only laughed. "I have no plans of drawing blood with something as simple as a knife, Cadet. Remember the last time you bled for me? Remember what I used?" Reaching over to throw the boxers aside, Sarge grabbed a pair of canes. One was a thick white plexiglas rod, the other, a thin bamboo switch. "Remember, Cadet Jackson? You said you could take what ever I gave. You even claimed you wouldn't cry that night, but I guess you overestimated yourself." Coming around the front of the stocks, he lowered his head to look Jackson in the eyes. "Think you're any tougher now?"

Terry took the plexiglas rod from Dar, and stepped behind the prisoner slave. "What do you think, Sarge? Straight to the cane, or the luxury of a warm up with the cat?" His hand stroked through his beard as he smiled at the bubble bare ass positioned before him. Sarge grunted and threw a deerskin flogger to his partner. "Thanks Sarge. Why don't you help him count them out?" He started practice swinging just above the cadet's back.

Dar forced Jackson's head back against the headboard with the palm of his hand. "Listen up, runt," he snarled at him. "My partner Doc is going to get you ready for me, but he loves to play hard with little punks like you. So if you start thinking he's being rough on you, just keep in mind that he's just the foreplay here. Every time that cat whacks your pretty ass, you are going to count the stroke and say 'Thank you Doc.' Understand that?"

"Yes, Sergeant Vlengles, Sir!" Jackson replied. Dar left Jackson's head drop, and cued Terry to begin.

With a fast crack of the cat, Terry landed two fast blows across Jackson's ass. The Cadet screamed in surprise and pain, then began to curse. Dar let his hand slam across his prisoner's face, restarting the blood trickle out of the lip. "That's not the right expression, boy! Let's hear it now!"

Jackson sputtered and cursed Sarge and Doc again. Doc used the moment to bring the cat down again, hard. "Damn you!" screamed the Cadet from his restraints. "One two and three, thank you Doc!" He twisted in the unforgiving stocks.

Terry laughed from behind the slave's view. "Sorry boy," he smirked. "The third one doesn't count. That was a motivational hit. Keep up with the count from here on." He pulled back and let a fresh blow crack across the cadet's cheeks.

"Ow!" Jackson screamed. "Ow! Three, thank you Doc."

Terry and Dar laughed aloud. "If you would have picked up on your lessons at the Academy that quickly, Cadet Jackson, you might not have been thrown out," Dar sneered. "Now let's get them right all the way through. Doc, continue the disciplining of Cadet Jackson. Make the count to one hundred."

"My pleasure, Sarge." Terry took another near miss swing above the cadet's back, and said, "You may bleed for Sarge later, but you will scream for mercy from me first." The next swing brought out the first touch of red in Jackson's ass. "Let's hear'em, boy!"

With each blow Doc delivered, Cadet Jackson kept the count. By thirty, the red was full and bright. The dark red appeared after fifty, and was turning purple by seventy. Jackson was also losing control of his voice after the purple grew deeper and darker, and as Terry predicted, he was begging the men to stop before the count passed ninety.

Sarge only laughed as he put the tip of the bamboo switch across Jackson's lips. "Oh poor slave. We aren't even halfway down with you yet. I haven't even taken my first round at you." He pressed his face against the Cadet's. "And believe me? You'll know when I get going."

Jackson wordlessly spit in Dar's face.

Dar stood with a shout. "Oh, poor poor slave. That was your last mistake." From the rack on the wall, Dar brought down a six foot whip. "Doc," he said, handing off the whip to Terry, "Give him the last fifteen with this. Oh, and don't worry too much about your aim."

As Dar wiped the spit from his face, Terry backed away from the slave and measured out the distance. He laughed again at their prisoner. "Well, well, Cadet Jackson. Looks like I do get to draw first blood." He watched as Sarge stuffed the spit hanky into the slave's mouth, and secured it with a short piece of rope. "I am going to like this part, boy," he said as he drew the whip back.

The first lash drew straight across the slave's back and pulled a thin slice through the skin. Gagged as he was, the Cadet's scream could only come away as a hideously loud muffled howl. Sarge put his face next to Jackson's as the lashes came in succession, whispering obscenely to his prisoner while scream after scream tried to break free. The blood was starting to run across the legs of Cadet Jackson, while Terry's expert whipping continued with Sarge keeping count.

"What do you say, Doc? You have two left. Where do you think they should land?"

Terry paused to think. Feeling the stark rage of sex running through his body, he lustily replied "One for each cheek. Maybe right up the crack." He wagged the whip in the air like a rat tail.

Doc slid his gloved fingers next to the tear filled eyes of Cadet Jackson. "Sounds good to me, Doc. Let him know how real Masters work." Sarge ran his tongue against Jackson's cheek. "Don't forget, Cadet. I have plenty in store for you after this."

Terry hauled back and let fly with two precise throws, one to each side of the prisoner's ass. The tip of the whip stung into the crack, just inside, enough to tear a tiny hole. Jackson's screams might have broken glass were it not for the gag, but the tears gave away just how much he was suffering. Doc was breathing heavy as he recoiled the whip for cleaning, and the oozing blood glistened like sweat from Jackson's back.

Sarge went across to a coiled hose and pointed it directly at Jackson's head. "Gotta clean you off for round two, son." He squeezed the nozzle gun and cold water blasted first into the side of Jackson's head, then tore across his back. The fruit of Doc's whipping began running to the floor. The mix of water and bright red Cadet blood swirled down the floor drain as Jackson twisted and struggled to dodge the force of the water's stream.

Once Dar decided their prisoner had been thoroughly drenched, he released the nozzle and watched as Jackson, dripping and defeated, began to shiver from the cold. "Doc, make sure he isn't going into shock, then let's take him down." Terry ran his hands along Jackson's skin, testing for cold or blue, but their was none, and despite his low sobbing, Jackson's breath was steady. Terry pulled the peg from the stock's hinge and loosened the slats securing their prisoner. "Let's cage him," Dar decided.

Jackson was lifted from the stocks, limp and shivering. Doc opened a steel cell and pushed Jackson on a cot with a blanket, and Terry slammed the door closed and locked it. "Think he's learned his lesson?" Terry asked of his partner.

Dar looked at him. His eyes were narrow and dark. "Not yet, Doc. He needs to know what eighteen years of rage feels like in one day. I want him to learn what happens to anyone who crosses me."

That was the look that Terry had seen before, and had scared him a few weeks ago. He may have dismissed it as too much beer then, but now he knew where that crazy anger stemmed from. Burning that kid's car wasn't a foolish act of recklessness, it was a displaced anger that Dar had buried in all the years since being forced from the academy. Terry knew he had to work carefully through this one, or Dar may just go too far. "Hey Sarge, his butt is ground chuck. I think we've given him enough for one session."

Dar turned and glowered at his friend. "After all this time, you think I'm not going to have my crack at him?"

Terry could see the red flushing rise in Dar's face. He had to think fast here, or Dar was going to really go out of control. "Ok, ok, you get your turn. After all, the little fuck screwed you good. But let's give him time to sleep this one off, and worry about his day with you while stuck in the cage." Terry hooked his thumb at the collapsed form of Jackson on the cot. "If he gets some time to rest up, he'll be fresh for some real pain in the morning." The comments had their effect. Even without Dar thinking straight, the idea of fresh torture made him calm down. "Fine," he said. "He gets a little healing time. Tomorrow, I am going to really put the hurt in him. I've been thinking about this little asshole's punishment for eighteen years. What I have in store for him they wouldn't even put on video."

With Dar calmed down, Terry felt a break in the tension. He knew that if he could get Dar asleep, he could come out here and let Jackson loose before sunup. He took Dar by the shoulder and said, "I got a few beers in the fridge. Let's down a few and get to sleep. He'll still be screaming in the morning." To Terry's relief, Dar smiled and said ok. After a couple beers and a snack, they retired to their beds.

Terry was deep in his sleep when he felt the warm sounds of a boy's begging, and the protests of submissive's collapse into surrender. The sounds of the dream were real, insistent, and very loud. But the sounds of submission weren't right in the dream, they weren't of the sensual giving in that would have awoke him in the morning with a hard on and a smile. Terry turned in his slumbers, and began the transition from sleep to wakedness. But the cries and protests didn't diminish. As his eyes opened, he realized that he wasn't waking up from the cries in his dreams, but from the very real screams of a man in distress. He leapt naked from the bed and saw a very wasted Dar dragging a screaming and fighting Jackson towards the door of a storage shed in the back of the yard.

Terry ran for the bedroom door, but Dar had it locked from outside. Turning back to the window, Terry could only watch as Dar dumped his prisoner on the ground, attached rope to Jackson's ankles, and hoisted the body off the ground with a block and tackle extending out from the shed roof. Dar had Jackson dangling from the front of the cabin, naked and exposed, screaming his ass off, and Terry could only watch as Dar kicked the slave's ribcage and ordered him to shut the fuck up. Dar disappeared in the shed, to emerge pulling a cart mounted with a pair of tanks, a bullwhip over his shoulder, and some kind of rag that he stuffed in Cadet Jackson's mouth.

"Holy Shit," Terry muttered to himself in a panic. "He's going to fucking kill the kid!" He threw the window open and began calling to Dar in an attempt to stop his friend. "Hey Sarge! I thought we were in this together? Come on up and unlock the door!"

Dar spun and looked up to the window. "Stay out of this one, Doc. I've been waiting eighteen years to teach this punk a lesson, and I ain't sharing this one with anybody!" He threw a wild punch into Jackson's gut and laughed as the suspended cadet spun on the chains. "You want to see what revenge looks like, you just stay right up there."

"This isn't it, Sarge! You waited eighteen years, but is it worth the rest of your life? You had too much to drink, man! Let him down!"

"Oh, yes this is, Doc. Once I'm done with my little cadet here, we'll go for a little fishing trip. With Jackson here as bait." Jackson began to struggle and cry out in gagged protest, but Dar drove another punch into his twisting gut. Terry could hear the air rush out of Jackson's lung from the window. The window wasn't wide enough to jump through, or he would've tried right then.

Dar was laughing again. "Hey Doc! Ever rape an upside down slave?" Dar swept his arms around the yard in another one of his grand gestures and added, "You got the best seat for the show!" Without any hesitation, he spun the naked ass of Jackson against his crotch and jammed his full hard cock into the hole without even spitting it wet. "Oh yeah! Doc you really should try this sometime...it's a high!"

Terry could feel his guts churning as he watched Dar's frenetic pumping of Jackson and the lust-howls that echoed off the fence. The fuck was so savage that Dar's load was shot in seconds. "Woo-HOO!" Dar bellowed, heartily slapping his slave's ass as he swung from the shed. "Damn. I gotta have one of these again sometime!" He looked up from the shed to Terry. "What do you think? Should I fuck him again and feed him to the fish alive, or just waste him here? I was thinking of whipping him till he was done...come on Doc! Help me out here!"

There was a silent panic from Terry's window. He knew that, if Dar started whipping Jackson, he'd rip the kid up like toilet paper. But if he told him not to whip Jackson, he may just kill him then and there without any chance to stop him. He remembered that the earlier caning could have torn Jackson's ass to ribbons but didn't, and he stayed conscious the entire time. He might be able to buy the kid some time.

"Give him a hundred more bloody fuckers, Sarge!"

The crazy laughter from the yard made Terry realize that whatever time he had wasn't going to be long. He heard the first crack of Sarge's whip land across Jackson and saw the body writhe from its helpless inversion. Terry looked around for something or some way to escape from the bedroom, there was a door to the hall and one for the interconnecting bathroom. With the hall door dead bolted, the bathroom was the only chance. The door between the two bedrooms was also locked, but Terry saw his way out. These door hinges were inside the bathroom. Even though he flinched each time he heard another whip crack, he knew that the noise meant he still had a chance to stop Dar.

He grabbed his Swiss army knife and began unscrewing the hinge bolts as fast as he could. The bottom hinge gave first, then the second. His hands were sweating as he spun the screw and kept listening for the whip. The pin from the top hinge dropped to the floor and Terry threw himself at the door with all his weight, only to have the doorframe crack and the door fall back inside the room on top of him. He threw the door aside and felt the pain in his left leg where the door had smashed his shin. He ran as fast as he could down the stairs and out the back door...only to realize there were no more whip sounds. "Darrrrrrrr!!!!!"

Dar, shoulders heaving and sweating, turned slowly to face his friend, giving Terry a glimpse of the bleeding chest and back of Jackson. Dar reached to a pack of cigarettes and lit one. "Don't worry Doc. He ain't dead. I wanted him to go out with a blaze of glory."

Doc ran to Jackson's slowly swirling body and dropped to his knees next to it, grasping it in his arms. Jackson's eye's were glazed, but he looked up to Terry with a semi-aware plea for mercy. He was still alive, but the bleeding from the beatings had taken the fight out of him. Terry could tell he was losing his will to stay conscious. "Jesus, Dar, let him down. He needs a hospital. We have to get him to a Doctor, now."

His back to the two men, Dar muttered, "he's not going anywhere." When Dar turned around, Terry realized what the two tanks on the cart were. They were Dar's welding torch, the one that he used to make his cages and other heavy metal toys. He stood in front of the entry to the shed and clicked the sparker against the nozzle.

"Doc," he said, "the saying goes that revenge is a dish best served cold. As far as I am concerned, I want my revenge very well done." He took and arcing swing of the flame towards Terry and Jackson. "Now get out of my way."

With Jackson's body in his grip, Terry held his ground. "Dar, no. It stops now. Put the torch down."

The blue flame waved back and forth, and close enough for Terry to feel the heat. "Doc, we've been through a hell of a lot together. I'm going to fuck this boy up, just don't make me fuck you up, too. Come on. Move out." Dar made a stabbing jab with the torch at the two men, and this time Terry smelled the singe of acetylene. Dar took two steps towards his targets. "Move it Doc. I'm going to finish the job."

Terry had one last option and he used it. Even though it may have meant more harm to Jackson, he hurled the hanging man directly at Dar, catching him off balance. Even drunk, Dar was still fast enough to catch himself, but Terry had the advantage of surprise. Pouncing from his position on the grass, he dove at Dar in a tackling move. The blow made Dar lose his hold on the torch handle, and fall back against the shed's door frame. He still managed to roll away from Terry and grab his bullwhip on the way back up. He tried to get a good swing in at Terry, but Terry was still able to dodge the throw. All the excitement had disoriented Dar just enough that, in his drunken state, he was throwing wild.

But Terry was still unable to get Jackson down from the blocks. Dar kept coming at him, and Terry was just not in the same shape as his former friend had kept himself in. Dar's lashes were getting harder and harder to duck, and one finally caught Terry in the hip. He stumbled down with a scream and looked up to see Dar pulling back for another throw. Terry tried to spin off and away, but the torch blocked him. The blow caught his wrist and blood shot up from the slice. Dar's laughter began to roar again.

"Thought you'd be the hero, Doc? I'm so fucking sorry you went and turned wuss on me." He threw the whip back in the shed. "Never thought I'd have to waste my best friend. Sorry Doc." Dar grabbed a short piece of rope and lunged at his adversary from the door frame. Terry braced his feet against the twin tanks of Dar's still ignited welder and kick pushed the cart with all he had left. The cart slammed hard into Dar, knocking him into a tumble. He grasped at the tanks for balance but that made him fall back through the doors of the shed and tip over on top of him. Terry jumped at the release on the block, and Jackson crashed to the ground. Terry could hear Dar cursing from under the cart, and as he pulled Jackson away from the shed, he saw Dar's hand reach out from the tanks and grasp at a shelf.

To his horror, Terry watched as the shelves fell down across the welder, smashing the valves off the top of the tanks. He had just enough time to throw himself on top of Jackson as the shed exploded. The fireball shot up through the trees and he heard several car alarms shriek out from the blast. He knew that firemen and cops would be coming any second, and he had to move fast. Hoisting Jackson into his arms, he carried him into the house and down the dungeon stairs. Dar had long ago built a soundproof isolation booth and Terry laid the limp but still awake body of Cadet Jackson inside and locked the box shut. Then he dialed 911 and was told that help was already on the way. Going up from the dungeon, he stepped out on the porch to wait.

There wasn't much of an investigation. The empty beer cans and the late hour gave the cops enough hints to list the death as accidental. Dar put down too many beers and had gone out to the shed to work with the welder, and had somehow pulled it down on himself. They never went into the basement, the upstairs bathroom, or as much as came back to ask Terry about a missing persons report filed by the employers of one Kevin Jackson after he failed to return from a trip to the mountains around the general area where his abandoned vehicle was discovered over a week afterwards.

Terry accommodated the Vlengles family's wishes and cleaned the house up for public auction, but there were a few things he kept for himself. On the morning after the fire, Terry stumbled down to the basement where the isolation box was still locked. He opened it up and found Jackson, still bound and gagged, but recovered, inside. Terry pulled the gag from his mouth. Jackson coughed and spit till his mouth was clear. Terry gave him some water.

"Thanks man," Jackson mumbled. "I owe you my life."

Terry thought back to the insolent comments at the flat tire that started this whole chain of events, and narrowed his eyes. He also remembered the insane desperate anger in Sarge's eyes the first time he heard the circumstances leading up to his retirement. "You owe me more than that, sonny boy." He moved his face to the brim of the box and stared into Jackson's eyes. "My friend was right about you needing punishment. He just went about it the wrong way. Thanks to you, he went crazy, and died. I think you owe us a whole lot more." He pulled a packing cart next to the box and tilted the container back against it. "This will fit in the back of my pick-up. I'm taking you over to my dungeon."

Just before the the lid closed out all light and the panic set in, Jackson heard the bearded man he was forced to call Doctor Sir the night before whisper to him, "Did you know the neighbors call me Doctor Terror?"

A VIEW FROM THE BLEACHERS

Sweat builds under rubber. Skin gets lubricated; muscles cool and senses fire up. Toxins are forced out of the muscles and into the bloodstream. Oxygen rushes into the lungs, stretching the rubber shirt out and in across the chest. That chest, devoid of hair. Is it shaved or does the boyish smoothness come naturally? If he does shave, how I'd relish the feel of my razor gliding through a fresh mat of hair, peeling back the layer of lime scented foamy cream. He'd lie still, just like ordered. Or else he'd be risking a nick near his nipple.

If he got too jittery, just the thing would await him in my bag of supplies. Four rolls of rubber stripping, perfect for holding a nervous rubber athlete to a locker room bench. Those black sexy shorts he's been wearing, as he concentrates on laps would disappear as the four-inch wide reels crisscrossed over his crotch. But not before I'd taken a moment to squirt a blast of wet lube under the waistband. Could he contain himself as the cool jelly oozed around his most intimate body parts?

Maybe he already poured some lube in his pouch before taking to the cinders. The crunching of his footfalls I can hear from my place in the bleachers, a sloshing crotch is too far in the distance. I entertain the notion that my rubber runner has already slipped a butt plug up his ass. He'd keep it in his gym bag along with a stash of athletic gear and sex toys, just in case opportunity knocked. That would explain his poise, his erect back, and shoulders to the sky stance. He leans into the curve as he rounds the track for his second lap. Watching him do his stretch-out pre-lap exercises worked one of my muscles. His arms pull hard on his running shoes, limbering those shoulders and that back, the bones of his spine pushing against his rubber top, the arching of his body exposing a crack of ass. Just those couple of inches makes me want to run my hands around his middle, savoring the slapping sound of an elasticated waistband. Letting his response figure into my judgment of his needs. How much more of a snap could he stand if I cornered him in a shower?

The athlete makes his way around the curve for his third lap. He's more than halfway through his mile. Sweat is prominently visible across his forehead. It beads on his brow, trickles down his neck and shoulders. By now the rubber outside his togs sparkles with perspiration just as much as the inside glides along the musculature of his body. Both his body and his rubber will need a thorough cleaning. Inside and out. If he surrendered to me in the locker room, I'd find a way to slip that butt plug out and insert a heavily lubed-up nozzle. Into the shower with him, restrained to the showerhead. I'd wash him down hard on the outside, and then give his inner plumbing a good, warm soapy cleaning. Maybe a second time, just for good measure. All the while his black rubber athletic gear would be hanging off to the side, drip-drying off.

Once his clothes and body had been thoroughly taken care of, I'd need to put something in its place. Either a latex-covered dick or a latex-covered fist. The rubber runner wraps up his daily mile only to find himself a completely different kind of ride. As hard as he is breathing on the track, we'll both be panting and sweating in a far more pitched fashion off it.

He's done with his mile, and he settles into the grass along the track for his cooling down exercises. He bends his legs into a butterfly formation, heels pressed against his balls. I get off my place in the bleachers and stretch out myself. He'll be back on the block tomorrow. And so will I.

I REMEMBER THE AIR RAID SIRENS

The skies would be bright and sunny, the air, crisp and stinging. We would sit at our school desks and stare out the windows, all childhood fascination and that tingling excitement of fear. Adventure waited just at the edge of the playground, the man by the monkey bars, could he be a spy?

That was the time I grew up in. "Duck and Cover" had nothing to do with birds and blankets, and every other Saturday, the klaxon atop the fire hall would send me and my parents down to the bomb shelter Dad had built into the back yard. Like so many families, Dad was completely paranoid of the "Yellow Peril" and the threat of Russians or Cubans dropping bombs on our little town of Parkersville.

The shelter was big, and to me, more fun than a treehouse could ever be. Let's face it, as any kid could tell you, we would just pound those commies into the ground if they ever got to OUR town. My friends and I had our own secret slingshot brigade, well practiced and ready to shoot rocks at the first Red to try to sneak up Main Street.

So Saturday after Saturday, my parents would run me out the back door and down the ladder, At the bottom, I was immediately was zipped into my child sized protective suit and my Mom and Dad got into theirs. I learned something else that summer...something about those suits got me "excited" in a way I didn't comprehend till later in life.

A ten year old has no idea what a fetish is.

Still, years later, I would crawl down the shelter ladder, get into my silver suit, and fantasize about being the last man on earth. Was there anyone to rescue me? Who would open the hatch? Would it be a tough American Soldier, who would break into tears when he found a real all American boy alive? Or worse! Could it be some Soviet or Nazi criminal who thought that I knew our Army's secrets? I often thought about a squad of soldiers, tying me to a tree and torturing me. I knew I would never break no matter how hard they whupped me, because everyone knows Americans never give up. It was also about then that I realized what kind of excitement these thoughts gave me...when I came in my silver suit for the first time. It was during a fantasy where some commies tied me to an ant infested tree and told me that if I didn't give up the secret codes, I'd be eaten to the bone.

I started going down in the shelter a lot more often, even after the air raid drills had long stopped.

I was 23 when my parents died in a car crash. How ironic...it wasn't the Reds that got them. It was some drunk asshole running a stop sign. We were never rich, but Dad actually knew how to save and invest. I got the house and the shelter, plus a more than tidy bank account. By then I knew that I wanted men for fun and sex, and that I liked my men tied, gagged and suffering for me. I had already slipped a few things into the shelter, some rope, chains and padlocks, but had never had the nerve to ask anyone over while Mom and Dad were still alive. But now I had the power to change all that. I traveled all the way to New York City to search for the things I really wanted and made that shelter into a nice place to contain visitors.

The best things I had I didn't even have to buy...Mom and Dad's safety suits were still in great shape. And of all things, a Zorro whip from my childhood was the first toy I ever used on a tied soldiers back. The Jersey Shore was full of them, disillusioned men who discovered that what they had in the war was nothing compared to what I could give them. The first one I ever tied to the ladder got my attention when he told me how hard he got when, trapped in a beach front, he escaped machine gun fire by the skin of his ass, running just in front of the stream of bullets as a plane strafed the sand behind his feet. He survived only by jumping from a barrier and into the ocean.

He told me he jerked off to the panicky memory, so I asked him how he'd like to be a prisoner for the weekend. He agreed...and I broke him. When we got to the shelter, I made him write down the "secret," put in an envelope and seal it. If he went 24 hours without divulging the contents of the envelope, I'd give him a fifty. He lasted eight. There were needles in his feet, fingers and balls before he finally told me his secret, of all things the simple slogan "Semper Fi."

But perhaps the best fantasy I made come to life started the day I walked past our local firehouse. After all those years, the towering yellow klaxon still had its perch on the roof. I had stopped to look at the old horn, when a younger hunk came out from the station and looked up to the roof aside me.

"Hard to believe," he said, "that people were really that scared of the cold war."

I told him how, when I was younger, that my parents were so terrified of an invasion that they had the bomb shelter built. This fascinated my new fire friend, as he had never seen such a relic. Hell, I figured he was at least twenty years younger than me. He'd be stretching it to remember as much as a fallout shelter sign. So I asked him to come over to the house and check it out. He was plenty happy to say yes.

He visited after his shift, and was very interested in my underground playroom, even if all the more interesting tools were hidden away. His attention really came around when he spotted the old silver suits hanging near the ladder's base.

"You know, I thought they only wore those in Power Plants," he said.

"No boy." I fixed a strong glare on him. "Imagine a couple of post war soldiers coming at you in those outfits. What do you think would happen then?"

He thought for a couple seconds and then replied, much to my delight, "They'd probably make me a prisoner of war, wouldn't they?"

New enthusiasm began bubbling inside. "What would happen if they caught you?"

"Hey," he replied, "you can't break a bulldog."

Time to go for broke. "Ever wonder how much you could take?"

Reward: "I could out last your worst. You and your army."

I started getting that wonderful hot juice feeling in my sac. "I'll make you a bet," I told him. "Three Hundred says you won't go 12 hours with me and my army here in the shelter."

"Like fuck I won't."

Goddam....he was mine.

I laid out the rules for the game right there. He was to show up at nine a.m. the coming Saturday in gear, but no shirt. He was to arrive with three code words in three envelopes. I would add one hundred to each envelope and he would seal them. For each code word I got out of him, I'd take a bill back, and any unopened envelopes, and their cash, would be his to take home. Once inside the shelter, the hatch was locked and there was no turning back.

"I can't wait to take your money, pal," he said. Damn cocky bastard; a hot fireman with dreams of being a marine and not breaking? It was going to be fun listening to him scream.

He showed up Saturday looking even hotter than I thought. Oxygen mask, bare chest, hot, compact bod...an inquisitor's dream. Meeting him in one of the protective suits, I handed him the three bills, he put them in his envelopes and I licked them shut. What I didn't tell him was my friend JB was going to be in on it. He came out from behind a shed in the other silver suit and grabbed my fire friend by his arm, holding him in place. "Meet the army, fucker," I snarled at him.

I grabbed his other arm and we began forcing him towards the concrete hatch. He tensed up, and started to kick and fight. He had no idea how much that turned me on...but I had to give the punk one last chance. "Still want to prove what a tough guy you are, soldier? Another two feet and you lose the option."

"Fuck you, commie prick!" he yelled from behind his face screen.

Perfect. JB and I drove him down the ladder and into the shelter, and I locked the hatch behind us. JB threw him to the bench and raised his hood. "NAME!" he shouted.

"Fuck you," our gas masked prisoner shouted back.

I slammed my fist into the prisoner's gut. "Yeah Mister Fuck You? How about the rest of your name?" I slugged him again, harder. I'll name you myself then, you are now scumgar. Got it slug?"

"You got nothin'," he snapped back.

This time JB slammed his gut. I grabbed a role of tape and began fastening him to the ladder, till he was wrapped in a tight black cocoon, with his balls open to my hands. A clutched them in my grip and crushed hard. All scumgar did was grunt. "Oh, you are gonna scream, fucker. How many needles can go in here? JB?"

JB knew what I meant. With a low laugh, he opened a box and showed scumgar an old fashioned sewing needle. "There are 120 in the box, scumgar. Think you're up for ten dozen?" He thrust the first needle into scumgar's leg, and he let out one grunt. Think you're a tough guy? You're a pincushion pussy, fucker."

Second and third needle, opposite legs, climbing up scumgar's legs. Fifteen and sixteen. Little more than gasps, Seventy to seventy-five. Little trails of blood against the black tape. At Ninety-nine, it was like a ladder leading to the balls, and our P.O.W. knew it.

"You wouldn't dare..."

JB answered that question with one quick thrust of the 100th needle. And finally, a scream to break cinder block. I laughed out loud, and scumgar passed out.

"Fucking pussy," said JB in disgust.

I laughed again. "Not this one. One hundred needles and he barely grunted? This grunt is gonna be a tough one. Get the copper thread."

When JB handed me the thread wire, I ran it from the floor and through the eye of each needle, criss crossing the length of all one hundred piercings, and ended by slipping it into needle one hundred one.

I set a candle on the floor below scumgar and broke smelling salts under his gas mask. "Wake up asshole!" He screamed again and then began fighting in the tape and ladder, only to feel the needles digging deeper. He stopped cursing and glared at me.

"One hour in fuckhead. Want to give?"

"Not a chance, pig"

"One hundred needles so far. How about One Oh One?" With that I jammed the last needle and thread into the head of his cock and listened to the wonderful screams of agony and howls and curses.

"You fucker, you'll never get away with this!"

"And what makes you think so, scumgar?" J.B. asked. "You break the bet now and you lose more than just money."

Scumgar panicked. "You said no damage! Let me out! Fuck you, I quit!"

I grabbed his facemask and shoved my face into his. "One needle in your dick won't even leave a hole. I got a power drill. Want to try that? Now talk or shut the fuck up!" Scumgar went ashen, and silent. "Good soldier. You know what we want. So give it up or suffer. JB, match?" JB handed me a box of Diamond Kitchen Matches and I struck one at scumgar's feet. The candle flickered to life, with the flame dancing at the tip of the copper thread.

"Listen up asswad," I sneered at scumgar. "Copper conducts heat, and that wire goes into the eye of all 101 needle leading to your dick head. How far you gonna let it climb?"

Scumgar's eyes lit up. JB and I sat across from our prisoner and watched as the wire grew shiny as the heat creeped up towards the first needle. We chuckled as the glimmer worked its way through the first hole, and the needle began conducting the heat into scumgar's leg muscles. First there were little more than grunts and groans, but increasing in volume as the heat shine worked up, needle by needle, searing the tape on scumgar's legs. JB and I moved in closer as the needle wire warmed up to the needle in his balls, waiting for the first wince of real pain, and we were soon rewarded. "Ahhhh! AHHHH! ARRRGGHHHH!!! Make it stop, make it stop! Fuck! Make it stop!"

"Talk, scumgar! Give it up! It just gets hotter! Give it up!"

He thrashed against the tape and ladder, screaming and cursing, begging! It was a sight to see; yet he still wouldn't let go of the first piece of the code. It took a couple more minutes, but he finally cracked.

"Fuck!" He screamed. "Spiderman! Spiderman! The first envelope is Spiderman! Let me out! Fuckin'a, let me out!"

JB responded by throwing a bucket of ice water on scumgar's legs, effectively dousing the candle and frosting the wire. He opened the first envelope and looked at me. "Spiderman," he said.

"You worthless weak little shit," I bellowed at scumgar. ""One hour in and you already cracked? How the hell do you think you'll survive the next eleven? Give it up now and the torture stops!"

Scumgar shook his head weakly and muttered "Fuck off."

Time for round two. J.B. and I cut scumgar loose from the ladder and stripped the tape away from his chest and jeans. The glue pulled at his chest, ripping the fine hair away with a satisfying amount of struggle from our prisoner, until JB rolled him onto his stomach and I tied his wrists together with a long coil of rope.

"Think it's too much rope?" I whispered into scumgar's ear, "Think again." Carefully, slowly, I began wrapping the rope around his wrists and coiling it up the length of his arms, pulling it tight as I wound upwards. Scumgar began to notice the pressure as I moved to his forearms.

"Christ don't break my arms! Stop!" he begged and cursed and struggled, so I paused to let him absorb his situation.

"Your arms won't break," I told him. "Your elbows will come apart very painfully and your shoulders will dislocate, and it will hurt worse than a bitch." I pulled the rope just to lift his arms up and watch his grimace, and hear his yell. "You know how to stop it, fucker. What's the second word?"

From his position on the table, arms pulling together and away from his back, scumgar stayed tough. "No! No! I won't do it!" He tried to roll, but screamed as the rope pulled him back. It was making me hard as hell, and I could see JB poking from his suit. I took mine off and pulled around to face scumgar, showing him the bulge in my crotch.

"What kind of torture would this be, fucker?"

"Jesus Christ! You're fags! Let me out NOW!" He began to thrash in the ropes again, even with the agony it caused.

"You're a prisoner and a pussy boy, scumgar. Do as we tell you and nothing goes bad. Now start telling me the codes and your pants stay on." Spit flew from scumgar's mouth and just missed my face.

"You're gonna scream like a drag queen, shit head," JB warned him. He picked a blowtorch of the floor and ignited it. Scumgar began screaming for help, and I backhanded his mouth.

"You think anyone can hear your sorry face?" I squeezed his jaw and smeared the blood from his lip. "I can burn your feet off and no one would know. JB?"

He lifted the blowtorch on the table where scumgar could see it. "Which end first?" he asked.

"The cut." I replied.

JB turned the flame at scumgar as he began screaming again. God, was I precuming through all this. JB took a cigar from the table and put it in his mouth, lowering the business end of the torch at the edge of the table. As scumgar watched the flame turn up, JB took his cigar to the flame and let it catch. He set the torch down and cut off the flame. Blowing smoke in scumgar's breathing tube, he chuckled..."the cut end. Always light the cut end." We broke into loud laughter.

"You're fucking crazy! Let me up, you're fucking nuts! Keep the money let me up!" He jerked and rolled, pinching his arms, and screamed in agony again.

"Oh no, that would spoil the game, now wouldn't it? Besides, if you are tough enough, you could still go home with two hundred." I lowered my face to his mask and squinted into his eyes. "But I doubt it."

I started coiling up his arms, squeezing them tighter and tighter, and enjoying the delicious screams of our little sack of scum. But scum or not, this fucker was tough. I had his arms all but yanked from the sockets and he still refused to talk. I decided to stop with the arms, but not to untie them.

Still lying face down on the table, I pulled his gas mask away. The smoke from JB's cigar curled out and he coughed like a horse. "Still think you can outlast us, scumgar?"

He sneered at me. Through his smoke filled gasps, he snarled, "I told you, bulldogs don't break."

"Bulldog?" I snarled back. "Those screams sounded more like an alley cat than a bull dog. You're a pussy boy, scumgar. Remember that blowtorch? I'll have the next word in thirty minutes. JB?"

JB lifted a chair with a metal seat next to the table and we lifted scumgar's ass into position. I took the tape again and spent 20 minutes tightly constricting his body, crushed arms and all, against the chair. JB took his cigar and this time flicked his ashes into the gas stream, sparking the hot blue flame. A metal pole protruded from the back of the chair and JB let the torch blast against it.

"It's a dull metal, scumgar. It takes a long time to heat up. It also takes a long time to cool off. The longer you wait for the second word, the longer you get burned. Give it now and the flame goes out and no hot ass for you. Get it, fire boy?"

"We're past thirty minutes, old man. I'll still be here when you check the clock."

"Oh no, scumgar. Thirty minutes starts now."

He couldn't see the flame this time. But it wasn't long before the first tingles of fire began to singe his ass.

"God damn, this will kill me! Let me out. This isn't fair!"

I could see the sweat beading on his forehead, and I also saw the erection in JB's suit. My suit was already off, and scumgar was certainly not oblivious to all 9 inches of man rod aiming in his direction. "Word number two, fucker. Fifteen minutes to go."

"Fucking bastards! When I get out, I'll have you killed!"

"Who said you were getting out? In fact, I think I'll MAKE you do the full thirty." With that, I took an oil rag from the shelf and crammed it in scumgar's mouth. An extra turn of the tape sealed it inside. "Scream for me, fucker," I whispered to him.

Scumgar obliged, whether or not he wanted to. The hot seat got more and more painful, and the howls behind the tape were louder than most men can unleash without their mouths stuffed shut. Twenty minutes. Twenty-five. Twisting, arching, fighting in the coils of tape. Twenty-nine. I gripped the edge of the tape. "Thirty!" I bellowed and ripped the tape off his mouth.

Scumgar spit the rag away and continued his screams. "Fuck! Fuck! I would have told you! Fuck! Let me up!"

JB went at him this time. "Say it, fuck face."

"Christ! Superman! Superman! Let me up, God damn you!"

I turned the torch away from the conducting bar, but didn't undo any bindings. "JB?"

JB went to the table and cut the envelope open. "Superman," he announced. After JB handed me the second hundred-dollar bill, I took a surgeon's knife and stripped the tape from the chair. Scumgar all but erupted from the grate, revealing a bright red criss cross pattern across his ass. He fell to the concrete and screamed again as the ropes jerked his arms once again.

"I feel sorry for you, asshole. You are so pathetic. JB and I thought we were in for a challenge, and we're barely five hours in. So you know what? We're going to have a little pity on you." I started uncoiling the rope from his arms, and JB opened a small door in the wall of the shelter. "We're going to stop hurting you for the next six hours. In fact, you'll have a room all to yourself."

I hoisted his unbound form away from the floor and towards the small hatch that JB had opened. JB and I began forcing him in, feet first. "It's not dark in there," I told scumgar. In fact it is furnished with five halogen bulbs, and a stereo system so you won't be all alone. There's also a microphone in case you get bored and want to drop the third word on us. By the way," I paused to hit a light switch, "the lights flash."

Scumgar struggled feebly as we shoved him in the hatch. As it closed, the furnace like lights came up all around him. We could see him on a small monitor, but given the confines of the space, there wasn't much to watch. I stuck a CD of Black Sabbath's first record in a disc player and hit the play/repeat button. Even if he could get through six hours of Ozzy's doom and death preaching and the sequential light bulbs without breaking, he'd still come out one fried cookie. JB and I had something else on our minds....lunch. We figured that, as it was two o'clock, if we were hungry, so was scumgar. Isolated in a box with little more than an empty stomach and heavy metal, those hunger pangs would kick in quick. We exited the shelter and went in the house, where we sat down to a pot of my spaghetti and a monitor of scumgar trapped in his little space. As we ate, we watched. We turned on a TV and watched the Mets. We chatted about work. We waited for a sign from our fireman pig.

"You know," JB mentioned during the game, "we're being soft on him. Had really been in a war situation, we'd be breaking bones by now. You think he knows?"

I snorted in disgust. "This punk is watching to many movies. He thinks he's fucking Rambo on the torture table. All he knows about the cold war is Reagan was president, and there used to be something called the Berlin Wall."

"Let's do him."

I was startled at JB's sudden turn. "You mean kill him?"

"No...rape him. I want to bust my nut." JB smiled evilly.

I loved it.

Right about then, a moan came from the monitor. I think it was about the fourth repeat of "The Wizard." About three and a half hours, and he was starting to lose it. I flipped the two way speaker set and asked, "Ready to give it up?"

Weak but solid, scumgar grunted back. "Never."

"See you at eight, fuckhead." JB and I sat and watched some sm porn vids. Scumgar just kept wailing.

Seven thirty finally rolled around, and JB decided it was time to bust some ass. We went back outside and down the bomb shelter ladder. We could hear the moans even before we switched on the shelter's monitor, but no calls for release. JB began to arrange the table for our final act, positioning restraints at the corners of the table and at the base of the legs. When he was ready, I killed the lights, music and opened the hatch. I grabbed scumgar by his hair and jerked him out from the box, and he screamed in surprise.

"What's the matter punk," I asked him. "Not ready to come out?"

I jerked his limp ass to the table and we spread him, ass up. His wrists were shackled to the corners, and his legs were bent off the table's edge. I positioned myself in front of him and began to snarl at him.

"You know what else armies do to prisoners, fuckface? They tear 'em new assholes. They gag mouths with hard man cock. You want us pulling a job on you? You'll be limping till next week, punk. What's the third word?" I watched as JB stood behind him, rubbing his cock with lube.

"Go to hell, fag," our scumgar muttered.

Just like that, JB rammed him. Scumgar let loose one wild fucker of a scream, long enough for me to shove my cock down his mouth. We stood there, pumping like horny curs, getting sweaty and hotter, and watching that muscular body struggling between us. Even with his attacking first thrust, JB was pacing himself, and so was I. He had a silky throat, massaging me perfectly, and I could feel the warmth starting to squeeze tight in my balls. I pulled out of scumgar's mouth and put my face next to his. "Give it up."

"You go to hell and you die."

I looked a JB and our eyes met. "Switch."

JB pulled out and brought his dick, brown from scumgar's shit, around front. And just as brutally as JB had entered scumgar's ass, I was inside. JB met the same wild scream by ramming his dick into the mouth. He took intense pleasure at hearing scumgar gagging on his own scat. "You can still stop this scumgar," JB told him. "Show me you're ready and I won't cum in your pussy boy mouth."

From all the noise I thought scumgar was going to puke, but he managed to keep JB in with out tossing. Pretty damn good cock sucker for a straight ass, I thought. It made me even hotter knowing this white-hot ass was probably virgin, and I could no longer stop myself. I shot red hot cum up scumgar's ass, grunting like a bull...pulse after pulse of shot. All JB needed to hear was me orgasming and his load let loose, too. Scumgar fought to spit, but JB ground his cock and hips into scumgar's face. That load wasn't going nowhere but down.

I heaved myself off and JB finally pulled out, gasping. "Give it, fucker. Say it now!" he bellowed.

All scumgar did was lay there and pant. There was something a bit off.....and that was when JB saw it.

"Mother fucker! Look under the table."

When I did, I was completely off guard. Pooling on the floor was a lake of jism. Scumgar had shot!

I spun to the front of the table and backhanded scumgar's face. "You liked that, didn't you queerboy!"

A low laugh from scumgar's stretched throat. "I always have, asshole. Time's up. I won." He chuckled again. "Bulldogs don't break."

"There's fifteen minutes left, you fuck. You aren't done yet." I turned my face to JB. "Tub! Now!"
As fast as we could, JB and I unshackled scumgar and refastened his wrists behind his back. JB lifted a metal grate from a table, and we force jammed scumgar into an antique 1850's porcelain bathtub. As JB slammed the grate down and locked it shut, I was spinning a valve connected to the shelter's water storage tanks. A stream of stale water began to flood the tub. Scumgar began to scream.

"I won, fuckers. Let me out, damn you, let me out!"

I sat on top of the grate and stared down into those fear stricken eyes. "There's still ten minutes. This tub fills in lees than five. How long can you hold your breath, fuck head?"

Scumgar was thrusting his body against the grate as the water flowed around him. JB was laughing at the screams...and I just kept my squint straight into scumgar's eyes.

"Say it now! Say it now or start swallowing!" Water was up against the outline of scumgar's face, and he was unable to keep it from running down his mouth. More screams, more curses. "Four minutes, drowning man. Think you can drink four minutes of water? Give it up!"

One more spit of water out of his mouth, the suddenly "It's Batman! Batman! Stop the water, turn it off. Turn it OFF!!!!!!"

I jerked the drain plug out and the water began draining away. and JB went to the table to open the last envelope. He looked at me and said. "It's Batman."

Without opening the grate. I looked down at scumgar's wet, trapped hot body. "Two minutes, loser. You could have been the first, but you couldn't last 120 fucking more seconds. What a piece of shit. Comic book heroes,

for Christ sake, Not only that, you lied to us. You wanted to get fucked."
"Yeah," he said from the tub. "But you almost blew it. You won. Now let me out."

I looked at JB. "What do you think JB? Liars go free?"

JB was already mounting the ladder. "Two hour penalty for liars," he said, climbing.

The thought of another P.O.W. rape was already filling my balls. "I think my partner's right. You didn't give full disclosure, so the rules change. So long, scumgar."

I began to follow JB out, and we both could hear "No! Don't leave me! Nooooooooo!"

SMOKE & HEROES

Ever since I was a boy just a few blocks from the Firehouse on Main Street, the sound of a clarion made my heart race. I'd jump out to the front porch and watch as the town Fire Department would rush to the shining red trucks and then speed off to whatever destination needed their service. My boy-self was so enamored by these men, heroes to me, that I would stop in the Firehouse on my walk home from school just to talk to these men, these larger than life individuals who would brave heat and death, all in a day's work.

They welcomed my curiosity, allowing me to sit in the front of a cab, playing with the station house dog (a Dalmatian, naturally), and giving me a soda from - wonder of wonder in those days - a vending machine with bottles.

Some three decades later, I've never "outgrown" my desire to be a fireman. In fact, it simply mutated into a desire for firemen. When my engineering firm transferred me to a small city in the Midwest, one of the first houses I was shown overlooked one of the city's firehouses directly across the street. There were a couple of other stops on the tour of residences, but they were superfluous. I had my balcony view of the station by week's end.

Auto-dialers and beepers have long since replaced the volunteer's clarion call, and fiscal realities now keep a small handful of full-time firemen on the payroll in anything less than a metropolitan area. Although it was just as easy to walk across the street and introduce myself, it was certainly out of the question to ask to be lifted onto the back of the ladder truck. But on those weekends when the trucks were pulled out onto the lot for their weekly washing, I'd be up on my balcony. I'd watch those shirtless muscular bodies, suspended pants pulled over thick rubbery boots, getting soapy and sweaty over hot red shiny truck metal. It would usually lead me back into my bedroom for a bit of auto bondage and a bottle of wet lube.

I'd perfected my favorite position long ago. Pulling my own green and yellow reflective boots over my feet, I'd lash them together with some cord, then pour some lube down my black rubber shorts before looping a set of chains inside my thighs from the upper corners of my bed. A masterlock would connect the two lengths of chain at my chest, then finally, my handcuffs in front of me.

From there, a preset timer would tick off the minutes while I'd entertain fantasies of rescue from smoke filled bedrooms.

Being played with while dangling off the back of a hook and ladder, or worshiping the boots and long coat of the men just across the street from where I lay, chains massaging either side of my rubber covered, pre-lubed cock and balls, I'd shoot an easy load or three into my shorts well before my self-imposed sixty-minute confinement period was up. Then I'd reach over to the bedside where the keys lay, undo the locks and cords, and perhaps go sun myself on the patio for a while longer while the truck and the men who washed it sat in the sun as they dried.

On a particularly warm June afternoon, two of my favorites were sitting on lawn chairs by the station's bay door. One was Ed, a Jeff Bridges look alike with a gorgeous, muscular chest and chiseled face. The other was Mick, whose gray grizzled beard and hairy barrel chest betrayed his Irish heritage, as did the remnants of a thick brogue. It must've been the first time I'd ever seen them at the station together. My mind immediately began spinning reel after reel of fantasy I'd scripted for each; my riding Ed's compact ass or my lips and chin, nuzzling their way around Mick's thick gray pelt, nipple to nipple, waist to crotch.

Inspiration like that didn't take long to result in action. I lay myself out on my bed, all the gear locked into place and imagined the two of them inviting me upstairs to the station's resting quarters, where we could enjoy the pleasures of a little man to man company. My rubber shorts were well filled when my timer rang, and I took my keys off the bed stand. The master lock came open easy enough, but when I went to undo the cuffs, the key just began endlessly spinning in the hole.

All those warnings about a spare key and damned if I didn't have one. I'm not a tool man; there wasn't a saw blade or hammer to be found in this house. Whenever I needed something like that, I'd just borrow one from across the . . .

. . . No! Absolutely not! There must be some way to work these open without embarrassing myself to Ed and Mick. The sole knowledge of the situation was humiliating enough. I made my way downstairs to see what, if anything, I had that might smash a cuff open.

Unfortunately, the carrot peeler and the can opener weren't it. I'd tried prying the cuff apart with a butter knife, but all I'd managed to do was to bend the knife double and nick myself. All that you may have read about picking locks with paperclips is bullshit, I blew an entire bottle of dishwashing soap trying to slip a hand through. Another hour ticked by and my embarrassment was starting to develop into a panic. It was getting closer to five o'clock, the shifts at the firehouse changed at six. At least I knew both Mick and Ed from speaking to them; I had no idea who'd be holding the fort for the next tour of duty. The possibility that there might be a bolt cutter across the street might be my only shot. I choked down my embarrassment long enough to slip a jacket over my shoulders and venture out the front door. Ed and Mick were still sitting in the station's driveway, relaxing in their plastic chairs, eyes closed to the afternoon sun.

They hardly even looked up as I approached.

"Hi'ya Jack"

"Hi Ed. Uhh, guys . . . I've got a problem."

Mick let one eyelid rise. "What's up?"

I shifted back and forth on my feet. "Can we talk inside?"

At this point, Mick and Ed looked at each other, then back at me. I was hoping I wasn't as humiliated looking as I felt. They continued staring at me, as if the explanation for this intrusion would start anytime. I was feeling more and more foolish the longer I stood there, so I finally poked my cuffed wrists out the front of my jacket just long enough for them to see.

Mick's big bushy eyebrows cocked. Ed let out one loud barking laugh. I turned 72 shades of crimson.

"Lose your keys, laddie?" Mick got up out of his chair and took me by the shoulder. "And now you need a cutter?"

"Yes . . . and can we please go inside?"

Ed this time. "Trust me, in ten years on the force, we've seen it all. I just never thought it was gonna happen right across the street. C'mon in."

Finally . . . the words I wanted to hear. Mick led me in and asked me if I wanted a beer . . . to relax, he said. To my surprise, he pulled my jacket off my shoulders, revealing my naked chest and my rubber shorts. "Well Ed, looky here. That's some interesting shit, laddie."

Now I was really embarrassed. Two men I'd secretly lusted after for the last year were going to run a humiliation number on me. All I could do was turn my head away and sputter excuses.

"Aw c'mon Jacky boy," said Ed, appearing with a long, evil looking red and black tool. "We pretty much had you pegged as a firebuff the week you moved in. Do you think we didn't notice you leaning off your balcony all the time? We just didn't think you were a kinky one." He punctuated his comment while snapping the bolt cutters in my direction. "I like those shorts, though. Now why don't you tell me and Mick just how you wound up with a pair of broken handcuffs stuck on you, then we'll decide if you deserve to have 'em cut off."

Mick laughed. "We mean the cuffs."

So I told them how I liked to watch them from my perch across the street, how excited real firemen had always made me, how I discovered bondage in college, and how my day had gone so wrong.

They thought it was hilarious.

"So a real fireman makes you hot and sticky, eh laddie?"

I muttered an embarrassed "yeah" in Mick's general direction, wishing they would just cut the chain on my cuffs and let me go home. What I didn't notice was Mick's chest, now just inches away from my face. "Why don't you show me just how much of a firebuff you are."

I hesitated as my embarrassment was still holding me back. Ed pressed his hands against my rubberized crotch. "It's okay; if you ever wanted a real fireman's nozzle, here's your chance." I let my tongue start exploring the broad range of Mick's chest. Ed's hands pushed at my cuffed wrists, driving them into his bunker pants and giving me my first chance to feel his crotch. I could feel his cock growing in my hands. "Besides," he added, "I always carry a spare set of keys."

There was a sudden cold feeling against my legs as the bolt-cutter tore at my rubber pants, dropping them to the floor. "It's alright," Ed told me. "You got a pair of hoses about to unroll here."

Mick had undone his fly so I could get a few licks at his cheesy, uncut Irish meat. I pulled back just long enough to ask if their tour of duty for the day was over soon. He laughed. "Ya'know Ed, the lad's right. If we wanna get our hoses cleaned, I guess we'll have to take him outside." He took a turncoat off the rack and lifted me into a standing position. Ed took one of his keys and undid my cuffs, and the two of them led me out back to the hose drying tower. As they guided me inside, I could see the long, swaying snakes of the company's second set of hoses, drying out from a previous run before some rookie would have rolled'em back up.

Two pairs of handcuffs were produced, and my coat covered body was left standing among the hanging hoses. "If you're gonna use handcuffs again,

Jackyboy," Ed said on his way out, "Get a pair you can depend on. Not that cheap dimestore shit."

"Yeah laddie," chipped in Mick, "and never forget to keep a spare key handy. See ya in twenty." They laughed as they shut the door behind them, on their way out. I was left standing in my fireman's boots and Mick's longcoat, hands cuffed to poles on either side of the tower. The smell of the drying hoses mixed with the long embedded smoke of the coat, giving me the beginnings of a very pleasant buzz. My crotch started warming to the situation.

Three decades later, these men were still my heroes. I could surely wait another twenty minutes.

Butch God Trilogy
Part I - The Tourist

He is my best friend.

So why am I here? We've known each other since college. During that time, I'd never suspected that he had a separate side to him, one that he'd never shown me. After graduation, we both took separate jobs in different cities. He took a job as a legal consultant in Seattle; I took a computer programmer job in Silicon Valley. I never suspected he was gay, even. He was just too straight for words, and I was too cute to be straight.

But a few years ago, after having not seen each other for years other than pictures, phone calls and the annual Christmas card, I found out that I was being transferred north...to San Francisco. I was in heaven! I was being shipped off to Gay Mecca! After telling some friends, Butch (it was what we called him, even in college), was the first person I called. I told him what was coming and was met with dead silence from his end of the line.

"Butch, what's wrong?"

There was another moment of silence before Butch replied. "I've been in and out of The City for almost three years now. My firm has offices there, and I was going to go there permanently as of next month!"

Now it was my turn to be stunned. Naturally, as soon as he got there, we hooked up for dinner. My jaw almost dropped when I saw him. Not only had Butch kept his looks since graduating five years ago, he'd actually bulked up more. Had I bumped into him at a club, I'd been all over him in a second.

We sat down and ordered steaks, and toasted our reunion in the City by the Bay. I asked him why he wasn't married and how he'd managed to stay in such great shape.

"All it does is rain in Seattle," he laughed, "so it's either work out or bloat from the boredom. As for the women, well, this may come as a surprise to you, but after a year of living in Washington, I finally came out."

"You mean, all those years we knew each other, and you knew about me, and you..."

"Like a three dollar bill."

"Why didn't you tell me?"

"Andy, we happened to become friends despite your being gay. You were a nellie as hell freshman and I had four years left before I got my law degree with an eye towards politics. At the time, nobody except my tricks knew, and they knew better than to out me."

There was something about the way Butch dropped that last line that should have clued me in, but it just skimmed right over my head at the time. We chatted about software I'd developed and how he'd risen to co-chairman of his firm for the next couple of hours, with me in awe of the aura he emanated. If he were in a courtroom with me, I'd definitely want this man in my corner. But when I asked him again why he evaded me for four years, he just smiled and said, "That's a topic for some other dinner. I'll pick up the check on this one, buddy."

That night, when I got back to my apartment, I realized what Butch meant by not wanting to come out to me in school. I was constantly hanging ACT UP banners around campus and my dorm was festooned with Erasure posters. Gay with a capitol "G". The first time Butch invited me, as a freshman, by for a visit, he'd moved off campus and had an apartment adorned with cowboys and scuba divers, and law books scattered everywhere. Very masculine images all, but in my limited scope, definitely not queer. I immediately wrote him off as a man who bragged about how one of his best friends was gay. And while I may have jerked myself admiring his brilliance and physique, it was from a touch-not distance. For the next four years we were thick as thieves and later I even realized that his BMOC friendship probably saved me from getting bashed. He graduated cum laude; I made Dean's list. I had a high enough GPA to get hired right off the bat, he got an entry level job at a prestigious law firm and almost automatically started scaling the ranks. I developed patents, he collected promotions. All to meet again here in California five years later! Within weeks, it was just like old times. We'd go out to dinner, talk about the stress of our jobs, eat a good meal, and maybe stop off at each other's homes. I wasn't surprised at the changes he'd made in his lifestyle, nor he with mine. His brownstone was tastefully decorated, but the cowboys and scuba divers were more erotic. My Erasure posters and had given way to movie and Broadway placards. Then one night, I believe it was our third after dinner drink, when he leaned into me conspiratorially. "Andy, do you want to know the real reason I never came out to you in college?"

I figured it was the wine...I was pretty buzzed myself. So I just rolled my eyes and asked why.

"Because while you and your friends were out dancing to Madonna in Mommie Dearest dresses, I was tying up men and beating their asses."

I 'bout spit my wine across the room. "You did WHAT?" I gasped.

It was the wine, because Butch giggled like a kid telling his favorite great big shock story. "By the time I was in high school and could see how some of the men in the stands were looking at me in my football and wrestling uniforms, I knew what I wanted from them. I wanted them under my control. And I was good looking enough to get my way."

"You mean you were fucking men in high school?"

"Not only was I fucking them, I had my first pair of handcuffs by the time I was a junior. One of the local cops gave them to me as a present for cuffing him and forcing him to suck me." He grinned a loopy grin at my astonishment. "I've had a thing for law enforcement ever since. One of my steadies through college was Murray."

"The security guard? That old bad ass?"

"Right. What a pig! Every weekend, Saturday at midnight, I'd meet him in the boiler room of the campus center. I'd tie him up, steal one of his cigars, gag him, and shove my fist up his old bad ass while smoking his stogie. Why do you think you guys never ever had one of your marches busted up big time?"

"You're kidding. The head of Campus Security..."

"Like a three dollar bill."

Butch picked up the check for that dinner, too.

That night, I had one of the hottest horndog dreams I'd had since I was a kid. I was back in college, and for the umpteenth time I was drunk and sitting with my activist buddies in Old Man Murray's office for chanting "Equal Rights Now!" by the library. In the past, he'd just fine us $50 apiece for creating a disturbance and order us back to the dorms to sober up, except this time, Butch barged in dressed in his full football uniform. Not the college Butch that was my best friend. A steroided, older super Butch closer to the one I'd just had dinner with. That was the Butch that shoved Murray down across the desk and handcuffed his hands behind his back, all the while glowering at me with a smirk on his face.

"It's more than a fine, this time, asshole." He jammed Murray's face into the desk blotter. "Isn't that right, pig?"

"That's right Butch, whatever you say."

Butch grabbed another set of handcuffs from Murray's desk and soon the old cop and I were cuffed together to a support beam in the security office. Butch yanked both of our pants down and began ramming his fist in Murray's ass while roughly jerking my cock. I woke up in sudden cold sweat, with a hardon that screamed for release now, right now, and when I finished it off, cum was flying out like I hadn't shot in ages.

I'd never had a fantasy like that before, never in my 28 years of fagdom! I had always secretly snickered at the leathermen in Pride parades, thinking that their gear was little more than their private extended Halloween, and that I, in my suit and tie existence, had gone far past them, the drag queens, and my old five nights a week of clubbing days. Yet here I was now, lying on a sweat coated bed sheet, my load staining my briefs, wondering what it would be like if a football stud would handcuff me for sex. I didn't know how open Butch was to talking about it, but as the cum started rolling off my hips and down to my bedspread, I knew I'd have to find out more.

It wasn't until two weeks later that we had another dinner, and I think Butch was taken aback by my sudden interest in his history. When I told him that, back in college, I used to think about him while jerking off, he laughed loud enough for me to blush. And when I told him that I'd had a dream about him handcuffing me and Old Man Murray, I could see the ego in his smile shining through loud and clear.

"So. Andy, you're not as straight laced as you'd like to make me believe?"

"That I would find you attractive?"

"That you would be attracted by power and control." He drew his steak knife through his dinner and watched the juices come out the slice. "Let me tell you what I did last weekend, the reason I passed on dinner. I was dressed head to toe in black, tight latex at a dungeon party. I scouted out the bottom boys and then parked myself off to the side and waited. Eventually, one of the cuter numbers came up to me and asked if Daddy wanted his boots shined. All I had to do was nod, and he was on the floor. I got a good overhead view of a young man with reddish hair and a tight ass licking his way up and down my boots all because I nodded at him. And after that, all I had to do was say 'strip' at him, and he was naked at my feet in seconds."

Butch took a bite from his steak as I sat there with my mouth turning dry. I couldn't deny it, my dick, under the table, was getting hard, fast. Butch swallowed his mouthful of steak and continued. "So I take him off to a corner and wrap two long pieces of rope around him into a bondage harness, and put a metal cage over his head. By the time I've got him the way I want him, if he so much as quivered that handsome chin of his, something sensitive would get pulled on. It's all so wonderfully interconnected. A handsome young stud, helpless at my hands, pleading with me to start working him over. So I lit a pair of candles and started dripping one hot drop of wax on his cock after another, and each time he flinched, something else got hurt."

"Hang on a second," I interrupted. "You mean you torture these men?"

"No, no, no...they come to me wanting something so badly that they'll beg." Butch smiled at me like a hungry carnivore. "Believe me Andy, I won't give pleasure to anyone unwilling to beg me for it. They tell me anything I tell them to say. If they want to get on my scenes, they have to start by telling me who they want." Butch halted his story and stared at me, knowing that I'd ask.

"What do you make them call you?"

"If they want to rock with me, they answer to the Butch God."

Even knowing Butch for all these years, and even as well as I thought I'd known him, I was finding all this extremely hard to swallow. Yet I had to know, the rock hard cock under the table wouldn't be satisfied unless I knew it all. "What did you do to the man you'd tied up?"

"I waxed him till he was screaming, then I made him change my name. If he wanted more, he had to worship the Butch Muscle Stud God. And he did...at the top of his lungs. I had quite an audience by then, people watching as he screamed in his ropes and cage, hard dick coated with candle wax, begging the Butch God for more. With me, standing over him in shining black rubber like a Greek statue, loving every second. Eventually I used up the candles, so I rolled him over and took my thickest paddle, beat him till I knew he'd be sitting on some bruises the next day, and then fucked his ass raw."

"And he wanted you to do this?"

"He came to me looking for it, Andy. If you could see how he lifted his ass to me, even though that motion was causing the rope around his chest to scrape his nipples raw, and begging the Butch Muscle Stud God to please fuck his pussyboy ass, you'd understand why I've always loved breaking men."

By now, my mouth was so dry that I had to take two big gulps of wine just to ask Butch another question. "Where do they hold these 'parties'? How do you get into them?"

"Andy, I'd love to take you to the next one. You could come as my guest. There's nothing to be scared of. No one does anything they don't want to, and no-one is allowed to force anyone into a scene they aren't comfortable with."

I was more than mildly intrigued. Actually, it was my dick that was intrigued. The rest of me was scared senseless. But I really wanted to know more. As Butch took the check again, I went home knowing that I'd be thinking of Butch standing over me, shiny, slick and strong in rubber, telling me to cum for the Butch God.

And so it went. We'd meet for dinner and exchange gossip, then Butch would tell me about people he'd played with or parties he'd gone to. Each night afterward, I'd have a massive orgasm thinking about how hot it would be to have Butch God putting clamps on my body or beating my ass with a leather flogger. My regular tricks and dates began to seem boring, but it was the reality of what Butch represented that kept me from accepting his invitations. Yet I couldn't stop thinking about it. I'd be at the movies, and afterwards in the restroom, while I was taking a leak, I'd imagine the man next to me suddenly slapping my exposed dick with a rubber strap, the way Butch had described over dinner the night before. Or wondering which man on the bus might secretly have a closet full of rubber, leather and toys ready for that night's play session. Or if somebody at work might have a chain locked around their balls under orders from a Master.

I was obsessing. I knew it, but still couldn't keep the thought of a weekend in Butch's ropes far from my mind. That week, at dinner, he smiled at me from across the table and once more extended an invitation to an upcoming event. "Butch, if you knew how much I wanted to go and don't want to go at the same time. But if I went, I'd just get in the way of the real players! All I'd do is be a fucking lookie loo, a tourist!"

Butch drew his lips together tightly. "You're already more than a tourist, Andy. Admit it, you want something like this. You always have. But it's only now, for the first time in your life, that you're close enough to the flame to admit to it."

My reply was as frenetic and sweaty as I was feeling. "It's not just that, Butch. I just can't picture letting anyone do those kind of things to me!"

"You're a bottom, Andy," Butch said, his smile returning. "Want to know how I can tell?"

I nodded.

"Because you just said you're concerned about someone doing it to you. Not 'you could never see yourself actually doing those things to another man.' You CAN see someone doing those things to you. You WANT someone doing those things to you. More to the point, you want ME doing those things to you."

"Yes! I mean no! I mean, aww Christ..."

"Andy, tomorrow evening my heaviest slave is going to be at the house for his regular training. I want you there to watch. If you think you're just a tourist, I'll give you a show that'll make your heart stop. You just call before seven."

My brain screamed no. My head nodded yes. I knew I'd make the call, well before the time he'd demanded. I swore I was looking into the smile of a shark.

"Good boy, Andy. Oh, and one more thing...when I answer the phone, ask for Butch God."

God help me, by seven o'clock, I'd called. I'd even asked for Butch God. He called me a good boy and told me to come over right away. I was out the door as soon as I'd hung-up the phone. The man I met at the door of the brownstone wasn't my friend Butch, the law grad from college. The man I met at the door was the Butch God.

He let me in, and I stood there in awe. He was wearing a tight pair of leather chaps, chains crossed over his chest. A black low cut rubber tank top pulled against his tightly defined muscles, reflecting back at me. He had on a Marlon Brando hat and reflective glasses. His short cropped hair no longer just carried an aura of authority, it also conveyed menace. It was only the voice that I recognized, as warm as the man I only thought I'd known.

"I'll only say this once, Andy. You are an observer tonight. This slave is my heaviest bottom, and he likes when I get real hard on him. You are to say nothing while we're playing...because as rough as I've ever been with him, he's never had anyone watching us. That's the twist in tonight's little game. And as cruel as it looks, remember that he comes to me looking for it. Understood?"

"Yes."

"Yes what?"

"Yes Butch God"

That predator smile again. "Good boy, Andy. You're catching on. Follow me."

Butch pulled open the door to a stairwell I'd never noticed before, and I realized that he had a basement. He led me down the steps and turned on the lights, revealing every tool and toy he'd ever described over our dinners and then some. Standing in the middle of it all, looking like my most wicked dream come to life, my best friend turned to face me. "Clothes off now."

I stripped. Butch handed me a bottle of talc and a pair of rubber pants. He covered my legs with the powder and chuckled at my difficulty at pulling the pants up my legs. He threw a pair of boots at me and watched as I clumsily laced them up. Then he reached into a closet space and withdrew a huge leather garment that, as I stared at it, recognized as a straitjacket. For the first time, I hesitated. Butch could sense it.

"Don't worry Andy," he reassured me. "I know how these work, and I promise you that I won't pull it all the way tight. Now relax."

I did as I was told, and Butch kept to his word. My arms wrapped around my chest as he pulled each buckle into place, and although he didn't crush me inside the thing, I certainly wasn't going to get out of it. Then he pulled out one thing that spooked me more than anything else. A rubber hood. Butch took two palms full of talc and began massaging it around my head and neck, all the while telling me what a good boy I was being, and that I was finally getting to see what the other Butch did best. And although I didn't realize it at the time, I wasn't going to hear my name for the rest of the night.

He pulled me over to the stone wall of his dungeon and threw some rubber padding across the floor. As he lowered me down to the cool cement and rubber, he explained the night ahead once again. "I'll be gone for about an hour picking up slave. When I get back, I'm going to give him one good wailing, and remember, boy. This is the slave I treat the hardest of any of my men. You'll be safe here till then."

Butch walked up the stairs and I heard the door latch behind him. As I sat there on the floor, confined and with my cock already rumbling against the rubber pants, again I had to ask myself. Why was I here?

Butch God Trilogy

Part II - The Slave

He is my Master.

That's all I've ever known him as. For the last two years, he's been the only man I've seen in that capacity. It's the way he wants it. I answer only to Butch God, and he has the right to come in or out of my life anytime he wants. Ever since I gave him a complete set of keys to my apartment and car, he knows that he can walk in on me and I'll be there for him. It's taken him almost two years to get me to this level, and believe me, it hasn't been easy. Yet no matter how hard I try, or how far he pushes me, angry or scared as I may get, I just can't make myself quit.

No one else gives me what Butch God does, and no one I've ever met has even come close.

I should have known him as trouble from the first night. It was over two years ago, I'd just got done on my shift. I work security for a housing firm here in the city, which consists primarily of cruising around during the day and chasing unruly kids around at night. That Saturday night was just bad shit all the way around. I had to break up two parties for noise, call in for back up on each, make three arrests for D&D, and put up with drunk assholes yelling threats at me while SFPD hauled them off for a night in the tanks. So I was hot, sweaty and really in need of a drink. I didn't even go home to change, which is unusual for me, I just went straight to the bar in uniform. If I'd've been caught, I would've been fired, but that night I didn't give a fuck.

I go full uniform into the bar and order my beer. My eyes were adjusting to the light when I noticed him staring at me. I'd never seen him before, and

I thought I knew everyone that came in here...but he was just too much to miss. That night, he had on a tight rubber tank top, a chain body harness over that, heavy rubber pants, a black motorcycle hat and, even in the dark of the bar, mirrored shades. And something else. Late as it was, on a Saturday night with drunken leathermen getting stupid with their beers, he was drinking a mug of cranberry juice. He didn't take his stare off me and I wasn't about to drop my eyes, either. I mean, who was this man? He was so well muscled and so perfectly hot that he made me nervous. His stare was so close to arrogance that it made me want to go to him and lash out at him at the same time, and I'd only seen him for, what? Five minutes?

We continued playing eye games. Until finally, he made the next move. He nodded a "Come here" gesture in my direction. For all the thoughts spinning around in my head and all the thoughts I was having about what a beautiful arrogant prick this guy was...I couldn't stop myself. I went over. And the first thing he said froze me cold.

"You're not supposed to wear your uniform in the bar, are you?"

Oh shit, I thought. Busted! No wonder he'd been staring at me! He was probably on the staff of Metro! After having the shittiest night on the job in years, I was going to get fired because I was too damn lazy to go home and change. But fuck it. As lousy a night as it had been, I didn't care if I lost or kept the job. "No Sir, I'm not."

He smiled then, a multi watt smile that could've melted steel, or lured in an unsuspecting fish. "Didn't think so. Just get off work?"

I was close enough to him to get a better look. His body was so well muscled that the rubber shirt rippled across his chest and stomach. The chain harness followed the patterns of his shaved, solid chest, and those arms could've crushed bricks. I nodded and said "Yes Sir," almost like reflex. I figured him to be a live one, and was already betting he liked to top cops.

He picked up the juice mug and walked past me. "Patio" was all he said. Now I was having problems. That was spoken like an order, but there was no demand behind it. This bastard was giving me a take it or leave it and I'd barely laid a word on him. But after a quick look at all the other regs at the bar, drunked up like they always were on a Saturday, I didn't think about it all that much.

I followed him out back to the patio. The second I was through the door arch, even behind the mirror shades, I could feel him sizing me. That chin, that profile...there was something there that was more than perfect. There was power. I extended my hand, which he accepted and shook strongly. "Name's Kent." I offered, and I stood and waited. He just looked back at me, silent. That's when I realized that he wasn't concerned with my name or if I knew his. But I asked anyway.

He signaled for a refill. "If we're still talking twenty minutes from now, I'll tell you what to call me." The barman came back with more juice. "And that's only if we're leaving together."

That, as far as I was concerned, was enough of a challenge to make sure we'd leave at the same time. Which we did, after exactly twenty minutes. Whoever this fucker was, he liked to play mind games, and I was determined to keep up with him. I took him back to his hotel and followed him to his room, which was pretty damn ritzy. For a moment, I was concerned that he might have a companion...but then I realized that there was only one of everything by way of luggage. It was one of those three room suites that wasn't what you'd be staying in if you were flying tourist class, if you catch my drift. He dropped the harness off his chest and took off his hat, and sat me on the edge of his bed. He then stood in front of the mirror and flexed his enormous arms.

"What do you think of 'em?" he said, keeping his face to the mirror and his broad back to me.

As he continued his poses, I replied, "Incredible, Sir."

Still not turning to face me, he commanded "Duty belt off and put it on the other bed." I did as I was ordered while he continued with his routine. "You want a piece of this? I'll tell you once, fucker. I like it rough and I get mean."

Yeah, so do I. And how many times have I heard THAT one before? Still...."Yes Sir."

"You want to suck the muscles of this stud?"

I was starting to really think this guy was either the hottest thing to ever get me in a room with him or the biggest jerkwad I'd ever followed out of a bar. Still, I answered..."Yes Sir."

"Then get over here and worship the muscles on this Butch God."

I started undoing the buttons on my uniform shirt, like I was going to take it off, when he whirled around and roared at me so harsh like that I jumped. "Who told you to strip, asshole?" he thundered. I stood there, hands at my shirt, so shocked that I couldn't move or reply. He grabbed me by the collar and shook me like a stray dog. "Let's get one thing clear right now," he bellowed, still working me like a dog's towel. "You don't move or speak unless you're told to. You don't shit unless I order you to. You don't even ask for permission to shit unless I tell you to, am I getting through to your punk ass?" I could only nod my head through the violent shaking he was giving me. "All right then, asshole. Now start on my arms and don't move off till I fucking say so." He took his massive arm and smashed my face into the crook of his elbow, against a muscle so hard I knew that I'd better do as I was told.

He smelled of oils and tasted of hard work, just they way I love it. I ran my tongue eagerly across those muscular cords, all while he kept talking to me but not lowering his gaze from the reflection in the mirror. "You work hard, but I work more, got that, pig? You think you're strong, but you aren't tough...you wanna suck tough? Only the Gods are tough. From now on, if you want to rock with me, you call me Butch God. Got that?"

"Yes, Butch God Sir!"

He grabbed my head and shoved it against the cut of his rubber tank top.

"Chest!" Butch God commanded. I began worshiping that massive chest of his, again overwhelmed by the manspace of it all. I drooled, licked, sucked. I tried to bite, but I may as well tried to chew steel siding. Butch God's chest was shaved clean yet the stubble tore into my tongue like sandpaper and smelled of the oils of a European wrestling arena. A leather gloved hand was slamming hard into the back of my head, snapping my neck and crushing my face into his hardness. I was getting scared, but couldn't make myself run. All I could do was suck his tit rings into my mouth and pull on the muscles of his pecs as hard as I could. I thought, from the way his voice continued bellowing his stream of "Work it, pig" commands at me, that I was satisfying this Butch God, this Master of Tops that before I could only have dreamed up.

Until he backhanded me so goddamn hard I spun around and crashed to the floor. He grabbed me through the back of my pants and threw me down over the bed. Now I was scared, and when he jumped on me and pinned my arms behind my back, I started fighting. But he caught me so off guard that, as his rope pulled tight around my wrists and my boots couldn't kick out from beneath his mass, in a matter of moments he had me where he wanted. My wrists were jammed behind me, my ankles were grinding together and his gloved hand clamped around my nose and mouth so forcefully that I could feel the inside of my lip splitting as I twisted to get out from under him.

"Fucking punk slave meat, that's all you are! I own you, faggot cock sucker, even if you're barely worth pulling it out for!" His hand yanked his fly down and I went 100% cold sweat on what he jerked to life in front of me. It was easily nine inches long, clean shaved, but the most terrifying thing was the piercing. I'd never seen anything like it, and believe me, I thought I'd done 'em all. Butch God's rings circled the head of his cock and then formed a triangular center up to and over his piss slit. It was going to be like getting rammed by a torpedo. I really started fighting him again, only to be met by another volley of head blows, while the other leather glove was jammed down over my mouth.

"Any attempts at screaming for help aren't getting out of this room, asshole! Not only do you get to taste a Butch God's cock, you're gonna taste some Butch God metal!" Just as fast as he could jam my mouth shut, he forced it open and that warhead monster drilled me. He grunted and shouted while I twisted and squirmed under him, choking and spitting, feeling metal bands crashing into the back of my throat as he bellowed and roared on top of me. I was scared half to death, I was hard, I jerked against the wrist ropes but I felt my tongue working as fast as it could to keep up...and with a huge roar, Butch God popped his load deep in my mouth. I could feel the sweat pouring off his body as he shook, salt running into my eyes as he trembled with aftershocks, all while his cum oozed past the metal helmet and was running into my throat.

As his cock began finally going soft and he backed off me, he was gasping. "Yeah," he said. "Yeah. You could be trained, jerk-off." He jammed a hotel room towel into my mouth. "Keep quiet, fucker, till I get dressed." His hot, oily sweat was combining with my fear stink, my uniform shirt soaking through. He rolled me over and I felt a small twinge of relief, thinking at last, as hot a session as it was, he was going to untie me and I could get the fuck out of there. Then he scared the hell out of me yet again. He pulled my wallet out of my pocket and started going through it. Jesus Christ, after all this shit, this psycho was going to rob me!

I couldn't even work up a plea from behind the towel, I was so wasted. I could only watch as he hitched up those heavy rubber pants of his while laying out my credit cards, my cash, my badge, my driver license and setting them out on the dresser. While I lay beaten on the hotel bed, he disappeared into the bathroom. All I could smell was our mixed sweat, his rubber and leather, and the stink of my fear. When Butch God came out from the bathroom again, he was dressed as I first met him in the bar, except this time I was more terrified than intrigued. He took a pen from the dresser and silently began writing on one of those yellow pads all hotels put out for guests...my credit card numbers, I was sure...I just knew that by the time the night was over, I'd be in a dumpster somewhere and he'd be riding my credit into another town for some new meat.

Then he really shocked me. He put everything back into my wallet except his notes and pulled me off the bed. I felt him jam my wallet back into my pocket as his chin pushed against the back of my neck. "Listen good, stooge fuck," he grunted. "Never go into another hotel room and let a total fucking stranger get you where I just had you. I could've wasted you with your own gun, you fucking idiot." He pulled the towel out of my mouth and I tasted blood from my split lip.

"Yes Butch God Sir."

He undid my ankles. "Stupid Cop pig slave meat, that's all you'll ever be. I've got work to do tomorrow, but I've got Monday night open." He undid my wrists, but didn't let go of my hands behind my back. As he shoved me towards the door, he whispered in my ear "You'll hear from me. Don't make any plans for Monday." He opened the door and knocked me to the hall carpet. "And when you hear from me, you answer 'Yes Sir Butch God,' fuckhead." The door slammed shut behind me, as I lay, bruised and broken, in the hallway. I pulled myself from the hotel floor as best I could and got the hell out.

Just one problem. After I got home, I cursed Butch God for kicking my ass, cursed myself out for giving in to the asshole, and shot a huge load thinking about the beating this hardass Master just gave me. Even with the implied threat and promise of him calling me out on Monday, I figured I'd seen the last of Butch God, and was both relieved and disappointed. Relieved in the fact that he frightened me, and disappointed because he so absolutely controlled me that I'd answer to him again if I ever saw him. I jerked off to the thought of that pierced metal monster ramming my mouth again Monday night.

By Monday, I was sweating. The smears under my arms far exceeded the day's heat or humidity. I was worried about whether my phone would ring that night. I rushed home and checked the answer machine before I even took my jacket off, before I realized that we'd never even exchanged phone numbers. Jesus, how stupid could I get? I had spent the day hoping and worrying, rubbing the bruise on my chin, hoping for a rematch, and he was jerking my chain...that fucker! If I ever saw him at the bar again!

Until the phone rang.

I jumped two inches short of the ceiling and had the receiver before my boots touched tile. "Jock strap, blue jeans, undershirt. Five minutes. There's a cab coming for you."

Silence. "Yes Sir Butch God." Disconnect. How the hell did he get my unlisted number, I thought. But I was at the door when the cab pulled up and asked for me by name, and so help me, I got in.

The cabbie drove me to the hotel and handed me a scrap of paper with a room number on it. When I knocked on the door, I heard a warm, regular voice call me to come in, but the man on the inside was a vision. He had on a uniform shirt, rubber gloves and the muscle rubber shirt from Saturday. He closed the door behind us and locked it, and I heard the commanding tones I'd sweated over Saturday. "Down to the jock, pigmeat."

I stripped and stood at attention before this man, who began exploring me with the rubber gloves and a narrow tapered crop. Fingers were sliding up the crack of my ass, the crop was jamming into my nipples. Butch God was inspecting me like some sort of thoroughbred. "Sir, how did you find my phone number?" I finally dared myself to ask. This foolish attempt to pose an unsolicited question was answered by getting the crop's handle bashed against the side of my head and that roar of a voice direct to my face.

"One! You call me 'Butch God'. Two! I ask the questions. Get it!" The silent inspection continued with me, naked to the whites of my jock, standing in the front entry of his suite till he was satisfied. His crop sliced air and slammed my hip. "Chair," he ordered, nodding toward a desk seat he'd placed in the middle of the floor. In short order, prearranged ropes had me harnessed in with extra duct tape around my wrists, chest and neck making sure that any movement was extremely limited. "Now," he said, pulling up a table, "I'll be generous and answer your question, then we'll move on to mine." He picked up an emery board and started filing his nails. "Since you were a stupid enough stooge fuck to leave your wallet out for me to go through, I just wrote some of the simpler numbers down, called the appropriate people that I work with, and collected all the pertinent information I needed. My turn now, cop pig. I need to know things about you that don't come out of some filing system. There aren't any right answers. After each answer, I'll reward myself. First question. Have you ever been another man's slave?"

"No, Butch God." No sooner had I answered the question than Butch God had run his nail board across my nipples in one fast stroke. I about tipped the chair over. For the first time since leaving the bar with him, he smiled. It was the kind of smile only a man used to total pleasure possesses.

"See? A Butch God doesn't need a dungeon full of toys to make a slave know his place. Second question. How many Tops have taken you as far as you need to go?"

Another answer, another question. Had I ever been kidnapped in a car trunk? Had I ever been shocked with a cattle prod? Each time, another stroke from his finger board. Each time reminding me that I was just raw meat, and before long I felt a trickle of blood threading down both sides of my chest. As the interrogation droned on, he didn't touch any other part of my body. Those two little spots, just screaming from the inside, hoping madly Butch God would turn his attentions anywhere else but there. No such luck. I was in screaming, fighting, crying, agony when he grabbed my jaw and squeezed it till I was staring him face to face.

"I own you now, pigmeat." Just like the first night, he stuffed a hotel towel in my mouth. "Time to christen the new slave vessel." While I watched, he poured something into a paper cup and threw it at my chest. I jerked so hard, that this time I did flip the chair over. I fell sideways to the carpet as the fire consumed my nipples and the towel absorbed the howl that broke in my throat. Butch God laughed. "Don't they train you idiot security cops basic First Aid? Always clean an open wound with simple hydrogen peroxide." Then he dropped his shorts and rubbed ointment between his rubber gloved fingers. I begged and pleaded as best I could behind my gag, sensing what was about to happen. As Butch God upended the chair to where my head rested against the floor and my wrists and feet flailed uselessly at the bindings, he jerked the gag out of my mouth and lowered his ass onto my face. "Get your tongue up there, slave," he demanded as I felt him settle into place. The ointment set my chest to fire a second time as the violent massage of my screaming mouth serviced this domineering madman. Right about then, I also recognized his truth. I wanted this from him more than from anyone else who had ever put a collar on me in some playacting scene, except this wasn't role play. This was as real as it was going to get. Despite my wracking pain, I drove my tongue as deeply as I could, and as I screamed for Butch God's mercy, his roars and shouts let me know the effect was just as hot to him as a vibrator against his prostate.

His load shot across my chest like the fire in the ointment, and without even realizing how close I'd been, I shot my own load into my jock. The chair went back up to its four legs and he stuffed the towel back into my face before disappearing into the bathroom for a shower. When he reappeared, he was dressed to go out for the evening, all rubber and leather.

"New orders, slavemeat. You can be my Number One slave if you want to, but you better know two things. I'll be telling you what to do every time I see you, and even when I'm not there, you'd better be ready for me." Butch God held a Priority Mail envelope in front of me and then stuffed it in my clothes pile. "If you can really take orders like you think you want to and like the pain pig I think you are, you'll put a spare key to your Master's new apartment and car in that envelope and drop it in a mail box by the end of the week." Butch God bent over the chair and his gloved hand slapped across my chest as he started untying. "Now get dressed and get the fuck out. There's a cab waiting."

By Tuesday night, the keys were in the mail. My life as I knew it was over for good. Two weekends later, before the sun came up, Butch God was in my apartment proving to me how much of a hungry slave I was. There were plenty of firsts in the coming months...the first time I was encapsulated in rubber, the first time he used my car to kidnap me in the trunk and drive me to where he wanted me. The first time I was ever fucked outdoors, the first time my back was whipped bloody, my first electrical punishment, my first tattoo. Butch God even showed up one evening with a tuxedo already tailored to my size for a night of theatre (with a hole cut in the pocket for a thumb to cock chain). I learned more and more to being under his ownership, and was endlessly amazed that he could still find ways to torture and privately humiliate me, which he zeroed in during the course of many sessions when he found out how strongly I reacted to it.

Which led to tonight. My guard shift was over and I was on my way home when I saw him. Butch God was standing at a post he instructed me to look at every night...a highway exit ramp sign near a public parking area. I turned into the lot as he came up to the car and ordered me out. In minutes, I was boot tied and hand cuffed in a canvas sack in my/his trunk as I felt the car go back out into the street. However long the trip took, I eventually felt this strong man carrying me over his shoulder and down a flight of steps, where I felt myself dropped onto the floor with a thud. Butch God pulled his sack open over my head and smothered my face with his gloved hand. "You're on best behavior tonight, fuckboy. I know you've never been done in front of anyone before, so tonight we try something new." He spun me around to face the wall of his dungeon, and my eyes began adjusting to the dim light. I could smell his sweat and rubber and it was already getting me precuming under my uniform. "My friend wants to know about Masters and slaves, and I want to show him how much I love a pigslave begging his Butch Muscle Stud God to give him what he needs."

I was kicked to the floor and when I looked up again, there was another man, in a straitjacket and hood, seated in front of me. My sweat went icy as I realized what 'something new' meant. Butch God was about to use me as a showdog, and if I didn't give 110% what he wanted, I was in for some serious hurt.

Jesus, how was I going to do this one?

Butch God Trilogy
Part III - The Session

This is how it is!

Right in front of me, my favorite pig slave. His feet, bound together, his hands, cuffed in front of his chest. He's halfway out of my canvas body sack, his cop uniform still sharp and smart looking.

Right in front of him, Andy, my best friend, who is about to witness his first real SM scene. Barely 30 minutes prior, I trussed him up in rubber pants, hood and a straight jacket, and told him I'd be right back with tonight's show. He'd been curious for months, so I'd promised him a display that would either convert him into a player or have him running for the door.

And I, Butch God, control it all. I grab the handles at the base of the canvas sack and dump slave to the floor of my dungeon. With one hard shove of my steel toed boot, he's at the feet of my friend, the tourist. Positioning myself with my knee high black boots on either side of his tight hips, I grab slave's shoulders and curl him back until he faces this hooded mystery man. It's time to make him work for his beating.

"Do you know what you are, slave?" I bark at him.

"Property of Butch God Sir!" he barks back.

"Does anyone touch my property without my permission?"

"No Sir, Butch God Sir!"

"What can Butch God do with his pig slave?"

"Anything Butch Muscle Stud God wishes!"

"And when can Butch God play with his dick suck property?"

"Anytime, anywhere, always and forever Butch Muscle Stud God Sir!"

"Damn right, suck face punk." I let go of his shoulders and knock him to the cold floor in front of Andy. "It's like this, stooge fuck," I start, taking a seat on a gym horse I favor for bondage and ass whippings. "My friend here has never seen a Top or bottom work out for real. You're already enough of a pig hole that you can't fake it, and he's known me long enough to know that I don't play second for anyone, especially some stooge cop like you. So this better not be the first time you go chicken shit on me or the only mercy you'll be seeing will be at the top of your Mercy Corner Med Center ER form." I give slave another solid kick to aim him in the proper direction. "Get to your first work station, pigmeat, and not another sound out of that punk mouth till I tell you."

As slave begins worm crawling his way towards the table I use for his warm ups, I remove a long plastic cylinder from my wall rack and hold it out to Andy with all the pride of a champion cattle brander. "This little baby is a cattle prod," I tell him. "Cattle herders use it on slow moving or especially stupid cows. Push this red button here..." I aim the business end at Andy and hit the charge. Andy jerks at the loud SNAP the prod makes, even though it's nowhere near him. "...and even the dumbest little dogie gets along. Watch."

I drop the prongs on slave's hungry ass and let it rip. slave screams and throws those cuffed wrists in front of himself as I lay the cattle prod on his uniformed ass one more time. "What did I tell you about noise, asshole?" SNAP! No scream that time. It makes me laugh out loud. "Catch that one, buddy?" I say to Andy. Like a good trainee, Andy says nothing but nods his head yes, just like I instructed him. And I know slave is getting scared about what else could transpire.

The second hit from the prod made slave haul ass. By the time I replace the prod to its proper place on the tool wall, he's lurched to the four post table I use for heavy interrogations. Grabbing him by the duty belt, I jerk him up and over the table top, undo his belt buckle, then untie his ankles. "You know your position, pig meat. Get into it."

slave stretches his boots apart as far as he can, and I rip his legs as far as they'll stretch. His boots get manacled as I round the opposite sides of the table and undo the handcuffs, rubbing slave's wrists before chaining them to opposite posts. slave is down tight and his ass is pointed right in Andy's direction. I want my tourist friend to get a good view of what happens next.

Stepping over to Andy with a black leather medical bag, I pick two objects out. "Just to show you that a real Butch God doesn't need fancy electronic gadgets to make a slave know his place, take a look at these. In one hand, a roller styled stiff plastic bristled hair brush, and in the other, a flat back wooden handled Fuller. Picked up both of these at a 99¢ store a couple of years ago. I know a bargain when I see one." I slip the flat backed brush into my back pocket and start rolling the bristles of the first brush around slave's shoulders.

The spikes of prickly plastic begin chafing slave's back. slave can see Andy watching him from the mirror and he knows his ass is on the line here. I muscle down hard on the brush, so the bristles stick slave like needles. He strains so deliciously that I drive him harder, knowing all the while that, no matter how harsh the sting, slave'll maintain obedience to his command of silence. He fears the punishment of disappointing me so deeply that he'd endure razor cuts rather than scream in front of our guest. It gets my Butch God monster cock throbbing against its metal helmet.

It's exactly that pig slave fear that I count on to open his pores. My hand slips under the elastic of his jock strap and I feel the wonderful chill of his sweat. slave has an attribute that I've never discovered in any body else. The man sweats ice. I've never experienced anything like it. The first time slave sweated one out with me, I thought he was going into shock. It wasn't until the next session that I realized slave was the embodiment of the cold sweats. Especially when I really fuck with his head. Get him real terrified, and you all but need a windshield scraper to bring him back to earth. Work his balls long enough and it's like beating a freeze pop.

As long as slave knew he was expected to perform for Andy, for this audience of one, he was going to be the iceman. And I was going to love every fist fucking second of it.

My glove smoothes the perspiration across slave's ass like it was cream. The prospect of raising some black and blue goose pimples from under my slave's salty smell makes Butch God muscle-sweat trickle against my own black rubber shirt. My torso begins to feel rhythm, my need for ownership and control rising to the helm. There may have been some sense of a script before bringing slave into tonight's show, but now instinct makes me reach behind me for the hard wooden handle. Time to put some color into my pigmeat.

From a shelf lined with butt plugs and dildos, I select a schlong as thick as a beer can and wave it towards Andy. The look from both their eyes is worth every court induced frustration from the week. I shift behind slave and let it slide across the cattle prod's welt, just to enjoy the silent twitch of slave's ass. But instead of crushing it between his hole, I move back to slave's mouth and rub it against those pouty, fuckable lips. "You're an asshole at both ends, pigmeat," I snarl at him. "Now suck it down for Butch God."

slave's mouth and throat expand as, quarter inch by quarter inch, he swallows the dildo to its filthy latex hilt. Spit oozes from the edge of his lips. I stand back from him, now slapping the hairbrush against my gloved palm.

"I promised my friend here a show of force, but I think I've shown him enough for the moment," I say to slave, my eyes on Andy. "So you're getting 120 seconds worth of hits. You drop that dildo and we start again. Got that, pecker mouth?" slave nods, his face glistening with cold sweat and drool.

I feel the intensity welling from behind my forehead as I take two other devices from my black bag and shoot a look at Andy. His eyes are giving me everything I knew I'd see by now, that primal mix of panic and desire. Maybe he thought he was just a tourist when he crossed my doorstep this evening, but right now I knew what he was wishing for, and it was more than just another story over dinner.

I unfasten the flap around Andy's skin tight rubber pants and slip the first device tightly under his balls, taking the time to turn the egg shaped vibrator on and listen to its hum. The effect on Andy is immediate, his already hard dick jumps and bounces with the extra stimulation. I pause to give his cock a real strong squeeze and give a long look into his lust filled eyes. "Your turn's coming, boy," I whisper to him.

The second device is nothing more than a simple L.E.D. countdown clock, which I set at 180 seconds and put in front of slave's face. Still slapping my palm with the wooden back of the hairbrush, I give slave a warning. "One hundred and twenty seconds, no warm ups or let ups, permission to cry out granted, as long as the gag stays in." The timer falls below the 140 second mark and I see slave tensing his ass muscles together in anticipation.

I let my bicep flex and draw back for the first swing. There is a moment of frozen forms, stilled, holding their places till the moment when I bark "Now slave!" and the hammer blows begin. I call this my two minute warning, hard and fast, a 120 seconds no holds barred hammering of my slave's ass. My eyes go nowhere else except for those magnificent cheeks, jumping, jerking, bouncing helplessly up and down, hearing the grunts and sputs as slave tries not to scream so hard that his pecker gag would fly away like a canister and he'd have to endure this from the beginning.

WHAM WHAM!

Color change is fast. Pink to red to flared crimson to a deeper darker red that I know will turn to bruised purple shortly after I stop. Wham Wham! Less than thirty seconds to go, slave's eyes pouring water from their tightly closed corners and his animal grunts filling the room. He hasn't lost the gag and I let fly with as many fast hard blows as I can fit in. Precision isn't the name of the game here. Speed of pain and wood on skin is.

WHAM WHAM!

The timer beeps its electronic stop and I pull back from any more strikes.

My chest is heaving from the windmill exhaustion of my arm, and slave's body is prone like a gasping fish. His ass is a myriad of reds and rising blues, a painting he will be reminded of seat first for days to come. I circle around and pop the dildo from his face and he sucks in air like water. As he cries silently, a sight that always makes a pierced Butch God monster cock stiff, I softly and sternly growl at him "Tell me what you are."

"Property of Butch Muscle Stud God, Sir!"

"God damn right, pigmeat." The restraints come off one by one and I pick him up and stretch him across the floor, on his chest, in front of Andy, ass canvas still where I can watch it. Prompting him..."You've got something to tell my friend here, don't you asshole?"

slave lays before Andy, who is now visibly squirming from the vibrating egg I've tucked under his balls and watching the slamming I just gave slave. I can see Andy's eyes, filled to their pupils with that look that tells me he's ready to surrender to a real Butch God. Just like I knew he would when I let him get a look at a Butch Muscle Stud God taking control...

And slave begins the story I've waited for Andy to hear.

"I was naked and asleep, and this was just a couple weeks after I sent Butch God a Master's set of keys to the apartment. I was completely passed out, when I felt a pair of hands grab my shoulders and force me down, pulling my head off the side of the mattress. Whoever it was hadn't turned any lights on, so all I could see was a big shadow over my head, and feel a pair of heavy gloves crushing my jaw, prying my mouth open. I was far too dead to recognize anything, and before I knew what was going down, my mouth was filled with dick and my shoulders were pinned, my head hanging down off the edge of the mattress, I was clawing and punching, but whoever was raping my face was too strong, and wasn't saying anything, just brain ramming his dick in and out of my mouth.

"Of course I woke up pretty fucking fast, and then I could smell the leather and rubber, and even though I was still fighting like hell, I knew. Butch God had decided to come by just like he told me he would, and that metal head was tearing up my throat again. All I could do was look up at this big muscle in the dark, and try not to choke as he fucked my face like some crazed animal. He let loose one mother fucker of a yell and shot his load so far back in my throat that I thought I'd pass out, and just as quick as he nailed me, he was done.

"He pulled his pants shut and grunted, and as he walked out, he told me I was total property any time he wanted, and I wasn't supposed to forget it. I was so stunned that all I could do was hang off the edge of my bed, Butch God's cum rolling out of my mouth and down my forehead...knowing that he wasn't fucking around. He owned me. I really wanted him to come back right there, as soon as he could. The next time I saw him, he didn't even bring it up. But we both knew. There wasn't any one else for me again, ever. Butch God was my new religion, and this bodybuilder was my God."

I'm so damn proud that, whenever I hear slave tell that story, I just want to take him off to a special room and fist fuck him clear up to the heart. Not tonight, though...I still have one more assignment for him.

I grab Andy's cock and pull it out in front of slave's fuck face, and much to my delight, Andy is swollen bright purple with the demand for needed relief. "slave's a damn good cock sucker now that I've got him trained," I tell Andy. "But he's still a stooge fuck, so tonight he has to go home without permission to cum."

"As for you, property pig, you get to show my friend here just how good you are. He's my friend, so he gets to shoot his load. You're nothing but pig meat, so you're going home with a sac full of jiz and you don't get to let it out while I've got guests. Now suck him off, fucker."

There's a red bandana in my left pocket, so just to give Andy something else to think about, I wrap it tight around slave's eyes. Lifting slave's face over Andy's cock and squeezing his jaw open, I drop his head over Andy's rod. slave is impaled by cock and has no option...it's suck or choke. Fortunately for slave, Andy's dick is smaller than mine and has no metal, so I know he'll give Andy amazing head.

Now I get a show of my own, as slave's head starts bobbing, giving Andy the blow job I demanded. He's an excellent cock suck slave, knows how to work his tongue and throat to maximum vuccusuck, and Andy's eyes are already starting to roll. I watch with fierce pride as Andy begins moaning, slave sucks and slurps, and I grab a handful of ice cold sweaty slave ass to inspire him to work that mouth. Andy starts moaning louder, overshadowing the buzz of the vibrator and the grunts of slave, and I can see him stiffening, arching, and then....releasing. I ram slave's head down hard into Andy's crotch, bellowing "SWALLOW IT, COP PIG! SUCK IT DOWN HARD!"

Now it's Andy's turn to suffer, because slave is hard-drawing every drop of cum from a super sensitive dick. Andy is squirming and whimpering, trying to back away from the face I'm driving into his groin with one hand, while my other hand iron-grips slave's bruised and pain filled ass cheek. My two dungeon dogs, totally under my control...if I still didn't have one more plan for the evening, I'd be jerking off in slave's face, slamming his face with my pierced monster meat.

Instead, I pull that cum drooling slave mouth away from Andy and tear off the blindfold. "Jack off when you get home, get it in a plastic bag and put it in the freezer. Next time I stop in to see you, it better be there." I re-cuff slave and start putting him in the canvas body sack to take back to the car. "As for you, my sick fuck tourist friend," I say to Andy, who is sitting, glazed and drained, "when I get back, we've got a few more things to act on before Butch God decides how soon you go home." Deep inside I feel my cock start firing up for a second go, because Andy's eyes are begging and fearing the salvation of this new icon, this Butch Muscle Stud God. With one fucked over slave sacked and hefted over my shoulder, I head up the stairs of my dungeon. Leaving a quivering former tourist to wait, wonder, and worry.

THE PRODIGAL

The click, the dial tone. Those are the last sounds I heard before commencing the drive. But it was his voice and what he said that stayed in my mind as I started south on I-64.

"You've been gone too long, son," he told me. "It's time you came home." Those were the words that clinged to my eardrums as I crossed the first of eight state lines on my way back. Back home, that's what you called it. The dark irony in my mind is the fact that I've never really had a home. I've called six states home, and this will be my, what? My fourth move into Los Angeles? Hardly what most men would call roots, but it is where so many things in my life began.

My first trip into leather, my first Leather Bar. My first bondage experience. My first trip into a real Master's dungeon. My first Master and his collar. Other things, too, like my first editorial position, my first attempt at a publishing company. Most devastatingly, my first really gut wrenching personal loss, and my first taste of failure.

There were a lot of men who figured that, by that point, I was a goner. A has been. Someone to get as far away from as possible. Not you Papa. No matter how stupid my behavior or the dimensions of the mistakes and actions, you never closed the door on me.

Once upon a time, you told me how bad you wanted to have a special place in my home, a clearly defined "Daddy's Room" to hang the flogger I gave you for your birthday. Did you ever know that I never gave any man an sm toy before then, and haven't since? I know that you are aware that only two men in my life have touched me personally and with such depth that I asked them to allow me to call them my Papa.

That is the power you have over me. That my move from the house to an apartment was the only time I ever found a man taking over me so completely. I remember as if it were last night, how I lay there, my clothes pulled away from my body, my limbs and mouth secured by the duct tape you picked up on the way over, your cigar filling the room with your scent, even before I had a chance to really unpack anything. My bed was not even properly made, yet it was your sperm that first struck the floor and sheets of my new home.

But that was years ago. When I announced my plans to leave California to escape the failures and ongoing difficulties of my dying business, you told me that it was not a good idea, and that I would never be at home in a city with out the activity of a major metro. And like you, many other men told me the same. "There is no leather there like there is here, timmy. As far as I am concerned, if you go to Kentucky, you go there to die."

But like so many other times in my life, I disregarded the warnings and left anyway. And like all those other times, you and the others were right. Damn it Papa, I missed you more than anybody else. When I stayed up desirous and lonely, it was you I dreamt of finally getting me into the total submission you say your capable of and dominating me straight through the floor boards. Naked and helpless, but calm and knowing, for you Papa. Prepared to take anything you decided was proper.

That was all fantasy till now. Drive, I said to myself, drive. Before the end of the week, I will be in a new place and the sign will be on the second bedroom door. I had the sign made in Indiana by a man who works metal to order. There was something of a release valve for me, because of his penchant for ass whooping. I paid dearly for this sign, Papa. His leather taws and plexiglas paddles left a week's worth of bruises, but I figured being tied for four hours in a metal shop while he alternately blistered my ass while waiting on customers was worth this kind of gift on my arrival. Will you bolt it to the door before you take me in for a welcome? Or will I be greeted passionately first?

Will that big black deerskin flogger be in your car when you meet me? All those emails you sent me, describing the adventures you have had with it, and the places the two of you have traveled. That hot Marine in San Diego you took control of late last year for instance, the one you said took three days of punishment before he broke under your demands, and the pictures of his ass, dark blue from those blows. How proud you were. The mention that you often thought of me as you were swinging the lashes at whomever you had for the weekend. And the irony again that I was never struck by the very gift I was most proud of handing you.

Soon, Papa. Very soon. I want to feel you pressing your full weight against me, that lion like look in your eyes (so many nights I looked into the dark and dreamed of them staring above me) before the take over begins. The ropes, the cigar, the lowering of your voice. The taste of your boots still in my mouth. The forbearance of the taste of your thick cock. My Daddy Niner. All I have dreamed about for almost three years again is my head blindfolded to stop my visions. Your voice against my ear, whispering one word.

"Son."

The chase is soon over, Papa. Will the catch be as great as both our expectations? Has the thought of me, finally home to stay and serving you in a manner most fitting, been one you dreamed of during the nights I was 2000 miles away? Was the memory of me, quivering and frightened the first time you surprised me with a dominant forced fuck enough to make you hard in the dark? Lord knows how may times I grabbed the bed posts and spread my ass wide thinking of that afternoon back then.

Those e-mails and instant messages were hot, too, Papa. Enough to make my hands sweaty with fear and lust, as you told me how bad you wanted to ram your cock up my ass, and to make me that sex slave you truly knew I need to be. Did you really mean that? Will Papa meet me at our favorite diner in West Hollywood for the breakfasts like the old days, or will he have something else in mind? I always secretly wanted you to have the spare key to the house, so that you could unlock the door and take me anytime for anything. I thought you did too. I pray you still do.

So how many state lines will it take, Papa? I must admit that this unrequited love I have held for you has given me a lot of fodder for my work. Each roll of the odometer feels like an increase in my testosterone level, like you are a magnet to my metabolism. The geography even bares a similar progression. The low mountains of older trees, the swampiness of the south giving way to the plains, dry flat but always rising. At each state line, another subtle change. Then from the barest twinge of the horizon, they arise. The Rockies show their first great peaks and the stirring begins. They grow in the windshield, a little at a time.

It builds and builds, just like my wants. And like these wants, I keep thinking that they can't grow any larger and they must be just a small ways off. Closer and closer, mile after mile, yet the peaks don't seem to get any nearer. Just greater. No amount of want or speed gets me any closer to those mountains. The grandeur of those sights, and yet the un-attainability of it.

Like you, Papa. Subtle, majestic, but never quite as close as we should be. When I finally reach their base, the rise seems insurmountable. It is a struggle to get past the interminable appearance, and downright frightening. But you know that the goal has never been an easy one. I should know. How many times did you keep me from giving up when I most felt like there was nothing left to gain? You would pull me against you and hold me like there was never an alternative. You demanded no more or less than my best. Whether it was your driving my face down your nine inch slick cock, or taking me to the woodshed about my painting, there was never a compromise. All challenges were made to overcome and dominate.

Dominate you did. The first time we ever chatted I wanted those boots in my face, and the voice behind the screen to make demands. I wanted that cock in my mouth, that hand slamming my ass, and the confidence to withstand you burrowing into me. As I reach the sign on the interstate that indicates I have reached the highest point on this highway in the US, I realize that the journey is all downhill from here. Though Los Angeles is little more than a day away, I can hardly wait. Coming down the pass into the sea of lights that cover the valley. Knowing, that with one more hill to climb, I will be in your valley. You and your flogger in hand, waiting for me, and I hope ready to have me again. There is just one thing in my moving trailer that I didn't bring from home. In the memory of that first night in my new apartment, when I made a stop for gas, I spotted rolls of duct tape for sale and bought two. Papa, I hope you're ready to use it.

A Slave's Training:

To Explode In Beauty

DAY 1

It is a Sunday evening when Master Dennis meets me at the airport. He is every bit as pleasant as his phone voice implied, and he walks me out to his car. There is a short length of chain and a padlock on the seat. He warns me that once the lock is closed, I am his property until we leave his house for the return flight. I nod and say "Yes Sir."

He chats as we drive to his house, talking about the flight, the weather until he opens the garage door for us to pull in. As soon as the door closes, his demeanor changes. "Out of the car, slave, and STRIP!" he commands.

I do so immediately and he takes the chain and locks it around my neck. "You understand that I own you, slave?"

"Yes, Sir," I answer. He puts my clothing in the trunk of his car, then tosses me a rubber jock strap. After I put it on, he also locks an ankle chain on both legs.

"As long as you are in my house, you are my slave. Understood?"

"Yes, Sir."

He laughs and leads me into his house, and immediately secures me to a kitchen chair with ropes around my wrists and chest. "Slave understands that every minute he's in my house slave will be in at least ankle chains and bondage?"

"Yes, Sir." I reply.

"Good slave," he answers back. He proceeds to ask me about my background, family, history, and also tells me more about his computer background. By the time he finishes interrogating me, he is ready for bed. "You will sleep in your ankle chains, secured to the bedpost. Understood. boy?"

I answer again, "Yes Sir." He unties me from his chair and I hobble as he leads me to his bedroom. He takes two lengths of chain and snaps the ankle chain to the foot board, and the collar to the bedpost. He curls up next to me and turns out the light as I lie helpless next to him.

"Don't worry slave. When we wake up tomorrow, we will begin your training."

When the alarm rings the next day. Master undoes the collar chain and forces my head over his cock. "You suck good, slave? Show me how you treat a MASTER's dick." And as he holds himself in, he forces me to work on him with my mouth and tongue. It lasts hours....and I am helpless to escape. "If I am not happy, slave....you will be punished. And it is NOT the kind of torture you will enjoy."

I redouble my efforts...it takes a while longer, but at last, he lets himself go and jams my face into his crotch. I am forced to drink my Master's cum. "That is your duty today, slave. Any time I order you to use your mouth, you will concentrate on my cock, balls, chest, feet, pits....where ever your Master commands." I cannot reply as my mouth is still gagged on Master's semi erect and dribbling dick. "But between sessions, I want you gagged and quiet. I want to test your ability at silence." Master gives me water to rinse my mouth and unhitches the cuffs from the bed. He leads me into his living room, where he makes me lie on the floor, hands and feet tied and a red rubber ball gag stuffed in my mouth. He proceeds to spend the morning watching TV and occasionally pushing me with his shoes.

Once the morning news ends, he rips the gag away and says "Pits." He lies on the floor and exposes his arm to me...and I worm over to the ripe, exposed manliness and begin to fulfill his command. He moans in pleasure as I work my tongue around the hair and muscle. He moans again and tells me that his slave will be expected to tongue bathe him every morning, and more as time goes on. I wonder what the more means, but before I can form any ideas, Master rolls over and commands me to please his other armpit as I did the first.

Afterwards, he lifts me to my feet and leads me to his bathroom. Master commands that I lay in the tub...and he begins to tease my jock strapped cock with liquid soap. "You do not have permission to cum, boy. My slaves piss themselves when they are in this position." The erection is giving me away, forcing the head to push its way out from the rubber strap, but I am powerless to stop this torture. The only way to escape punishment is to piss myself, fast! I force myself to ignore the pleasure of his torture and relieve myself all across my body, and Master laughs at the sight. He stands and let's himself go all over me, my Master's piss overwhelming and mixing with mine. "This is how a piece of property should smell...the scent of his Master!" He exits the room, leaving me to wallow in the yellow of the tub. After a while, he returns. He affixes a gas mask across my face, and then removes the ankle chains. "Can't risk rust," he chuckles and then hits me with a full blast shower. The water slams into my body; the mask holds my surprised yelp behind it. "You understand this, slave. If you are chosen to be my slave, you will spend days at a time reeking of my piss. All over your body...AND slave's mouth. Master likes slaves in their place. A slave's place is under my control."

He leaves me, tied and masked, in the tub.

I spend much of the day trapped there, where he comes in several times to piss on me, and once to cum on me in my helpless little space. "Slaves do not always deserve to eat a Master's cum, but there are times when it will please me to feed it to you."

He exits again. He is torturing me, using me, training me, yet so far without pain. I respect Master even more. His control is just as demanding as making me scream in agony, and he knows it.

Finally, he pulls me from the tub. I am cold and shivering. He likes that. He replaces the ankle chains and leads me out to his kitchen. "Dinner time, slave. Get under the table." Master serves himself and sets it on the table; he kicks his shoes off, and rips the mask off my head. "What better a dinner for a new slave than his Master's feet? Get to work, boy."

I dive to the linoleum, and as he eats I pleasure each foot, his heels, ankles, and ten toes. Master completes his dinner, pulls me out from under the table and unties my wrists. Master orders me to get on all fours, "like the dog that you are." He then takes the dinner leftovers and places them in a bowl in front of me, and commands me to eat.

"Yes, Sir, thank you Sir." I am truly grateful, having not eaten anything since the snack on the plane flight. I gobble eagerly, and he places a bowl of water next to the food.

"That is for thanking your Master, slave. I can give rewards when I am pleased, slave. Tomorrow, you will cry for me!"

Day 2

We went to bed in the same positions as the night before, my collar and ankle chains affixed to the head and foot boards of Master's bed. I drifted off with the thoughts of dinner and curious to what he meant by crying for him. It seemed like only a few moments later that Master's alarm clock raised its morning siren call and Master was slapping me awake.

"Yesterday was a get to know you day, slave. Today is the day you get to serve me. Go to the kitchen and prepare me two eggs, scrambled, two slices of toast with butter and three sausage links." Master disconnects the collar chain and frees the ankle chain and all but shoves me out from his bed. "Hop to it, slave."

I hobble to the kitchen and search his pantry and refrigerator till I find what I need and prepare exactly what he ordered. I take the breakfast to his table and he comes out. As he takes his seat, he orders me to sit on the floor next to him. "When Master is done with breakfast, slave is ordered to cook one egg to your preference and one slice of toast with no butter. No sausage. Slave will eat less than his Master till he achieves the weight Master feels is healthiest. The slave will clean the dishes and table, and report to Master's bedroom. Understood slave?"

I nod and say "Yes, Sir," and sit in silence until Master rises. He leaves the room and heads to the bathroom; I stand and gather the breakfast plates. My breakfast is prepared to his specifications, and I start work on the clean-up. Once I complete that chore, I march back to the bedroom, ankle chains and all.

Master has prepared the bed with four ropes to each bedpost, and he orders me to get on the bed. Once I lay in place, he binds my wrists to the corners, then unlocks the ankle chains and bonds my feet to opposite sides. Master has me in a secure spread eagle and puts on a pair of latex gauntlet gloves, stroking my stomach. "Today slave, we will see if you can be compatible with the kind of pain I enjoy inflicting on my property." He produces a ring gag and buckles it around my head, forcing my mouth open and vulnerable. "Are you ready for the rest of my breakfast?" Master asks mirthfully.

He moves to his knees and points his crotch at my face. I begin to struggle as I realize his intention, and Master laughs again. "All my slaves must learn to drink directly from my tap," he says. He pins me down and stuffs his cock into the ring, forcing my jaws open, and lets a torrent of hot piss explode down my throat. I have never been forced to drink piss before, and struggle to keep it going down without gagging or choking. Master seems to have a limitless supply, and for a moment I fear that Master will drown me if I don't catch a breath. But even he has his limit and I feel the torrent turn to a trickle as I gasp for air. Master is gasping as well, but not for the same reason as me. "That was good, slave, very good. Not a drop missed. You are already on my good list this morning." He lays by my side and sighs his contentment.

"Yes Sir, thank you Sir," I mumble through the gag as best I can. I am still making sure that there are no extra pockets of gold in my mouth, and swirl my tongue in the pockets.

"Good slave. You remembered to thank your Master when he gives you the gift of himself. Let's see how long that will continue." His hands pull the jock down below my ball sac, boosting it into a more handy position. He rises from the bed and pulls out a small wood box, opening it before my eyes. Inside is a series of needles, in various lengths and thicknesses. He removes the piss gag away from my mouth and replaces it with the rubber ball gag. "Of all the tortures I enjoy, slave; this is your Master's favorite." Master takes a short, narrow needle out and twirled it between the gloved finger and thumb. "This lets me get under a slave's skin, and to see what comes out from underneath. Are you ready, slave?"

Since Master has thoroughly blocked my mouth, there was no reply. "Good boy. Here comes the first." With no more warning than that, Master slides the needle into my ball sac. What ever noise I could have made is blocked by the sheer shock of feeling a needle pierce my groin from one side to another. There is no time to recover, as Master takes a similar needle and shoves it through my cock. This time there is no shock to stifle me, and I scream into the gag. Master's face lights up.

"Good slave. Express yourself for your Master." The third needle, a longer one this time, is jammed into my armpit, and I feel a warm spot of blood. The same feeling shoots through my other armpit, as Master gives it the same treatment. Now I am thrashing in my bondage, and Master pauses. "Struggle is good, slave," he says. "But not what I want right now."

Master's pause in his work is just long enough to produce four more pieces of rope, applying them to my knees and elbows, making it even harder for me to wiggle on his bed. Once he has me more secure, he again holds the box near to my face and pulls four more needles loose, and takes the gloved fingers to pinch my tit till the nipple is higher up. Master then rams two needles in an x pattern through the skin beneath. As my scream drowns out the pain, he repeats the procedure on my right tit. With two short pieces of rubber cord, Master loops the nipples below the needles, which thrust the pressure points higher, and with each twist, the more painful the position. This is beyond any threshold of pain I have ever known, and I begin to see the stars spinning behind my eyes.

"Don't worry slave," he says gently. "There is much more to come." He reaches under the bed and withdraws two white long stick candles. Master lights them and waves them over my chest. "I have to make sure the rubber does not slip off your needles, slave. Take a deep breath!" That quickly, my already distended tits are doused with flaming hot wax. My scream is clearly audible, even with the gag in place. But Master is merciless now, and he allows wax to pile across the rubber and needles, encasing them. He completes his handiwork, then moves to the foot of the bed. "Slave knows that the feet, although very sensitive to pain, are difficult to damage, don't you slave? That is why interrogators love to beat a prisoner's soles. He can be broken with little signs of his torture. I am ready to show you, slave." He lowers the lit candles to my feet.

Try as I might, there is no way to pull away from the pain. Master allows the flame to dance along the soles, and pulls back before a burn occurs. Then he comes in again, as I thrash and scream uncontrollably. At some point, I blank out and all the torture and helplessness turns into some kind of blurry time suspension. All I know is Master's voice goading me on and the searing pain in my feet, groin, pits and chest. It seems an eternity before I hear Master say, "Well, slave. It looks like you can cry when pushed long enough." He removes the gag and unties my legs, and dabs away my tears with a tissue. All I can feel is the heaving of my chest, desperately trying to fill my lungs with all the air I've lost from the screaming.

Master removes the needles from my cock and balls, and my armpits. I feel myself calming, until Master begins picking the wax at my nipples. The shooting pain again sends the stars in my eyes spinning around...and he grips the rubber cords and rips them away from the base of the nipples, sending wax flying. Without the gag, my scream rips from my throat, yet as loud as it is, I can still hear Master's laughter. "Better get used to it, slave," he growls. "My full time boy will be tortured daily. Do you understand that?" I am barely coherent now, and can only nod yes. Master then puts his gloved fingers against each tit and snaps the four needles from my chest. This time the pain is too great.

However long it took for me to come around, I do not know. But as I come back to consciousness, I realize that I am on the floor next to the bed, my ankles again padlocked in Master's chains, the jock pulled over my cock and balls. He hears me stir, and peers over a newspaper he is reading. "Ahhhh, my pet wakes up. Good. I need to go to the store, slave. Get up and come with me."

He leads me into the hall and opens a closet door. But there is another door in the far end that he also opens, and signals to me. "This is your hole, slave. Start thinking about the time you will spend here. If I leave the house alone, or I have guests, this is where you will be." He pushes me into the crawl space and I feel myself sliding into a rubber sleep sack. Master pulls the zipper up tight, leaving only my head exposed from the rubber encasement. He locks my collar to chains fastened to an eye hook in the wall.

"I will leave you here till morning, slave. I will be at the market to get some supplies for your play tomorrow. I hope you like camping, slave." The door to the secret compartment closes, and I am left in the dark to ponder and perspire.

DAY 3

I have no knowledge of how long Master left me in the space. I awake now to noises outside the wall of this closet cell. I wait even longer until a sound of a door startles my attention. Light floods into my eyes as I hear Master calling me.

"Come out slave, and get dressed." My eyes readjust from the cell's total dark. Master has brought my clothes from the trunk of his car. I look at the clothes and recall what he said on the first night, that I would remain naked in his house at all times. It can mean only one thing. Master is taking me out. He unfastens the lock to the collar and chain and unzips the sack, coated with my entire night's sweat.

I dress, as Master tells me that last night was an unusual thing for him. "I tend to like my slaves in the open where I can see them," he explains. "If Master has tasks in his house that do not require your participation, you may be tied to a bed, chained to a chair, or told to stand against the wall, but I rarely allow my slave to be where I cannot reach him, and perhaps feed him a taste of his Master. Understood slave?"

I respond obediently, "Yes, Sir." It is already obvious to me that Master would rather appreciate my actions than anything I have to say. He shows me one of the articles he picked up during last night's trip to the store. From the plastic bag comes a dog leash. He snaps it on to the collar's padlock and pulls. I notice that he has put on a pair of hip high waders.

"Come, slave dog," he orders. "We are going for a walk in the park."

I am ordered into the back seat of Master's car, and he disconnects the leash. "I am a private Master, slave. If we play outside of the house, you will be dressed as a companion. You are still my slave, but for all outward appearances, we are friends." We proceed up the street and on to an expressway, and on for several miles. Master takes an exit in a remote area and then turns off to a remote mountain road, then a fire road. There is nothing here except rocks and trees, and I begin to get nervous. If Master were to leave me here, would I be able to find my way out? As I think of what is happening he pulls over and gets out of the car.

"Get out and strip, slave." I hesitate for more than a moment, and Master turns. "Strip NOW slave!" He opens the car door and snaps the leash on me, and now I am scared. I fight back, but Master has me off balance. He knocks me to the ground and pins his boot behind my neck and yanks back on the leash, hard.

"What the hell do you think you are doing, you stupid shit!" he yells at me. I am twisting and struggling to get my neck out from Master's boot, but I am not loose enough. Master is still shouting. "I told you yesterday that I hoped you enjoy camping...are you such an idiot slave that you already forgot?" I realize Master is correct and fall limp. I am rewarded with a sharp kick in my ass. Master grabs my wrists and pins them with cuffs. "Get off the ground and beg me to not punish your sorry ass, slave, and do it fast or I am going to give you a beating that even your father wouldn't have forgotten."

Master heads for his car, and he opens the trunk. He is till shouting in anger as he reaches inside. "You are at twenty hard ones, boy. Right now I am not feeling inclined to be forgiving!" I struggle to my knees as Master turns around. He retrieves his hand from the trunk to show me what he has in his hand. It is a black, thick, single cord leather bullwhip. Master draws his arm back and makes a strong slashing throw. The air cracks thunderously. I am already to my knees. That sound almost makes me fall back. "Start begging for me NOW, slave!" Another crack of the whip punctuates his command.

I am so scared that I can barely open my dry mouth. The two slashes in the air from six feet of brutal leather cure that quickly and I stutter, "Master, please forgive this wholly unworthy slave for doubting your integrity and for the slave's foolish weakness of fear. Slave promises never to raise his hands in fear or anger to his Master ever again. Please, Master, do not strike this property in madness, please Sir, strike me all you want, but please, Master, only strike your property in desire and for your pleasure, Sir." I lower my head to the ground in penitence and wait Master's reply.

"Not a bad start, slave," he says softly. Master steps up to where my head rests in the dirt. "So far, you are down from twenty to five. What do you offer as a bargain to not receive a punishment beating?" Master drops the tail of his whip next to my head, and I swallow hard. "Your Master is telling you to suggest pleasurable methods to dismiss punishment strokes, slave. If I were you, I'd start thinking of something to say."

"Please, Master, piss in the mud at slave's face and make him stick in his mouth and drink of it, Sir!"

I hear Master unzip his fly. "Very good slave, that's two strikes off." There is a splashing sound and piss hits the dirt in front of me. It pools up and I watch as Master shoves his rubbered foot down, grinding the dirt and piss into a plate of mud. "Get your face in it, slave," he orders. I edge my mouth against the puddle and stick my lips to Master's sludge. He surprises me by shoving his mud covered boot down on the back of my head, forcing me down into the mud, crushing my nose and mouth in Master's slime.

"Do not ever disobey your Master's orders again, slave!" he bellows. "You are MY property to do with as I wish!" The stench of the piss sludge is setting off my gag reflex and I can barely breathe from the pressure Master's boot bears on my face. "You're down to two, slave. Can you stay down long enough to clear the debt?" Master pushes down harder; I feel my nostrils flood with piss and dirt. "One, slave! Obey!" I can't stop myself now; I am coughing from the dirt in my mouth. But the coughing and gagging only draw more sludge in, and I hear Master laughing as he grinds his boot again. "You are done, slave. Now get your ass over here and strip!" While I gasp and choke on the ground, Master unlocks his handcuffs. "Learn this lesson well, slave. Disobedience will be punished. All punishments can be negotiated. Also, if slave has something that he wants for himself, Master may agree to it if slave is willing to bargain for a trade." There is a very thickly trunked, dead tree a few feet from the berm of the fire road. Master motions towards it, and commands "Get next to that tree and lie down on your back! Now!"

I crawl toward the tree. But it is not fast enough for Master. He pulls his belt from his jeans and begins striking me across the ass and back. I double time my way to the tree, feeling the inflammation heat rising. Master jams me against it, back to the trunk. Lengths of rope are secured about my wrists, elbows and chest. Duct tape is spun around my forehead. Master gathers more items from his car trunk duffel bag. From inside, he removes two heavy duty lawn stakes and pounds them into the ground with a mallet. To these, he knots pieces of rope that he leads to my ankles. As hard as he can stretch them, Master spreads my legs at an angle that is tight and painful. My cries of discomfort are met with Master's smile.

"You sucked me off Monday, Slave. So you should remember how good your Master is at delaying his ejaculation. Pleasurable for me, torture for you. If I feel you are not performing at your best, I will give you a reminder to work harder. Understood, slave?"

My back is being scraped by the rough surface of the trunk, I figure it will be easy to concentrate on getting Master off. "Yes, Sir!" I bark in reply. Master says nothing, he simply drives is cock into my mouth and begins pumping hard. The dry cock catches in my mouth and I can feel a gag coming. I focus on driving every molecule of spit to lube Master's hungry thrusts, and even though he is driving me like a machine, I can almost handle him.

That mad thrust does not last long. Master is fully erect, and he begins his torment of slowing down to stave his payoff. I work as hard as I can with my head taped to the tree, as such, my ability to bob in and out is all but canceled. Now I understand Master's reasoning. I can't work his cock. He controls all the elements. All I can do is feel the bark scraping my back raw, and Master's pacing of his pleasure. He has made me little more than a slippery orifice to toy with until he tires of this torture and decides on his next course. It is taking him a long time to tire of this game, even withdrawing from my slave mouth to drink from a bottle of water. I follow the sun as it passes its peak in the sky, then as it moves westward down. Master still has me in this role as his open mouth, and seems to be unconcerned about the crampiness of my legs and the cutting of the wood into my back. His sole mission is to have the longest possible suck time he can manage. Even I am beginning to wonder how long Master can control his own ejaculation.

As the sun begins caressing the tree tops, it finally happens. Master's moans become louder, hoarser. He begins to tremble and I can feel the shivering in my mouth. "Take every drop, pig slave," he bellows. The cum fires out of his cock and into my mouth, and it is a huge load. I feel like someone has dumped a full carton of milk into my mouth all at once. I rush to swallow it down, even as I feel my cheeks swelling near the breaking point. The prospect of Master threatening me with his bullwhip saves me, I manage to keep all his cum inside, and the greater part of his massive load is already down. I wait for the collapse of Master's hard on and for him to remove himself from my face, but he doesn't. He just leans into me and the tree, gasping. I figure that if I had spent the entire day holding myself in and scraping a slave mouth raw, it would challenge my stamina, too.

I was wrong. He presses himself tight into my mouth again, and I feel his reason why. The warm taste of piss is beginning to dribble into my mouth. Those bottles of water were not to re-hydrate him...they were for this! The dribble turns into a thick stream which I again have to struggle to keep up with. For a second time I beat the urge to spit Master out and quit; and all the piss goes down. I clean the head of Master's cock with my tongue as he retracts into limpness. Finally, Master backs away from my mouth and beams a huge smile.

"Very good, slave! You took two very large doses of your Master and did not lose an ounce. I am very proud of you, my slave. But now there is a problem. I no longer am feeling horny." He moves to the stakes and unties my ankles. The relief is instantaneous, and I quickly pull my legs together to alleviate the stiff pains. The arm ropes and duct tape are also removed.

"No slave, your Master no longer feels horny. But your Master is feeling very sadistic. It is time for you to take your Master's lust for a man in pain." He turns me around and pulls my arms back again, forcing my chest back against the bark, which is now moist with the sweat of Master's near six hour blow job. My arms are fastened again, as well as my elbows and head with more duct tape.

My back, already raw and scraped from the tree bark, faces Master and I can only hear him. From behind me, he announces "I told you that I would not whip you as a punishment, slave. That did not also mean that there would not be a whipping." I feel a gentle slap as Master's bullwhip snakes lazily across my shoulders and draws back. "So far, slave has given Master his mouth for piss, slave's eyes have poured tears for me, and slave will now give Master another liquid reward. Is slave ready to give up his blood for his Master?"

I answer back with a hearty "Yes, Sir," but I barely have time. A slash of air barely warns me of the deep burning blow of Master's first strike. My cry echoes through the sundown. Master begins a fast series of strokes and my screams are indistinguishable from blow to blow. I have no idea how many times Master is ripping into my back, all I know is the heat from my back, and the coppery smell of the torn flesh's blood offering. Time falls out from me again and I am plunged into a world that no longer differentiates between torture or ecstasy, or between forced submission and willful service. I can only concentrate on the passion that is erupting inside my soul for the man who is guiding me through this mountaintop epiphany. However long that sensation could have lasted, Master recognizes the limit of this slave and I discover a warm hand across my shoulder. It is Master, whispering in my ear about what a tough little slave he has found, and how it makes him so happy that his slave will bleed for him and give into the gate between agony and revelation. He tenderly rubs salve into my shredded skin, all the while talking gently about how long he has toiled in his search for a boy like me. He undoes the ropes and lowers me to a blanket and tilts a water bottle to my mouth, the same mouth that has been rubbed raw by Master's cock, swallowed down Master's cum, screamed out for Master's mercy, and finally sobbed the words "Master, Master," over and over again. This slave mouth was given another gift from Master, the honor of his refreshment and care.

He allows me significant rest before handing me my clothing and orders, albeit in a softer tone, to get dressed. "When we return home, slave. We will go directly to sleep. You will need a long rest after this effort. I am proud of you." With a look in his eyes that is different from any stare he has bestowed on me all week, he reattaches the leash to the collar. I recognize the significance of the look. I feel an incredible rush of emotion, because what Master has inside those bright eyes of his, is pride. He closes the door of the car and commences the drive home.

DAY 4

When we went to bed last night, Master was very kind and generous to me. "A true slave sleeps on his Master's floor. Tonight you have earned that privilege. But you have earned an additional reward." Master placed a pillow and two blankets on the floor next to his bed. "Tonight my slave earns his doggy blankets." Just as before, though, my ankle chains and collar were locked to Master's bed, this time on the foot posts and head posts. My exhaustion from the day's intensity did not allow me to stay awake long, and I dreamt of Master's whips, rubber hoods and gas masks.

When Master awoke me in the morning, he was already unchaining me. "Breakfast, slave. You know the drill. Hop to it, slave."

I move to the kitchen and begin to prepare Master's eggs, sausage and toast. Despite the dull throbs that pulse through my back, I am feeling a sort of elation that has eluded me for quite some time. Once I finish Master's meal, I present it to him in his bed. He orders me to the floor. I sit still until Master completes his breakfast, then he gives me permission to make my own.

Once I have finished my meal, Master removes the ankle chains and orders me into the bathtub where he ties my hands. He positions me in the tub and tells me, "today we play target swallowing, slave. Open your mouth." I do and Master commences to piss. "Follow the stream, slave." He moves his cock back and forth, and the piss splashed all over my head. I do my best to follow the gold, but it is impossible. Master is laughing at my feeble attempts to comply with his order.

By the time Master is done, my face is completely soaked. Master does not give me the privilege of a shower, telling me he wants me to smell of him through today's lesson. "You are an immensely talented slave, you know that? So far you have drunk my piss and cum, and for your part, pissed, cried and bled for me. Today will be the last day of your training. Tell me slave, what is the one fluid you haven't dispensed for me?"

I think for a moment, than ask. "Is it slave's semen, Sir?"

"So intuitive! Yes slave, today you will show Master what kind of load you can shoot, and you will also learn the discipline and control my slaves must show to please me." Master unties my wrists and helps me to my feet. I step out of the tub and Master makes a command. "Bedroom, slave. And lose the jockstrap."

I follow Master into his room, and take off my jockstrap. He orders me to stand at attention. From a bedside drawer, he removes a small chrome and rubber device. He steps toward me and begins working on my limp cock, and I feel cold metal circling my shaft, repeatedly. The Master snaps what kind of feels like a cock ring. "Let me show slave how this works. I stimulate you by; let's say stroking your balls." His fingers begin a slow tickling under my sac and the pleasure stirs a response. "Now when that slave cock of yours gets too big, the metal rings will trap it and make it squeeze. Has slave ever experienced the seven gates of Hell?"

Master is right, as I feel the crushing rings confine my cock to the point of agony, and it instantly goes soft. "What I want from you, slave, is your ability to do as your Master does. I can hold back an orgasm for hours. The gates are a means to that lesson for you. But keep this in mind, the rings do not come off until you do cum. Now let's see how much you can stand. Get on the bed, slave."

I jump to the bed, and Master again ties me in a spread eagle. He adds the joint ropes as well, and even some more. He takes a package from the same chest he stored his Seven Gates in, and reveals a rubber hood. He pulls it over my head, and strips off the velcro blindfold. A rubber plug gag remains attached and fills my mouth. I can only watch as Master begins removing all sorts of devices from his cabinet the other toys were in, and lays them one by one on the bed. It is too difficult to see what all he is thinking of using on me. I wonder if he could actually use them all before tomorrow morning. Before he decides to start in on me, he needed to finish one more task. He has a federal express envelope he is writing on, and he exits the room briefly. When he returns, he is beaming.

"Let us get started, slave. Remember, the longer it takes you to cum, the more suffering you will endure, but the longer it takes you to cum, the more exciting your ejaculation will feel. Understood, slave?" I nod my hooded head and Master picks up his first toy. It is a dildo of some sort, and he gets a bottle of lube and begins to finger my ass. As much as I resist, he still force jams it into position. Then he does something else, a slight click. Instantly I feel a massaging of my prostate. Immediately I had an erection and just as quickly an enormous crush of pain! Even with that constriction of my shaft, it is difficult to force myself to concentrate away from the vibrating dildo and to focus on bring myself to softness again.

Master is pleased with the results. "See, slave? You can learn very quickly.

Now you will show me what matters most for you. The pleasure of self gratification and ending of your tortures, or holding back and submitting to your Master's orders." He leaves the room again, this time to the bathroom. From the bed I can hear him rinsing the lube from his hands, and when he returns, he has his rubber gloves from the first day. He leans on the bed and begins to give my nipples the exquisite rubbery massage that would, under any other circumstances, result in an erection. I am able to withstand Master's initial forays, but it is only a matter of time. My cock stiffens again, and the vice-like pain begins anew. I am trying to scream, but my stuffed mouth allows no release.

It is the ultimate reversal. My audition for a place in Master's home began with Master torturing me for pleasure. Now it is Master pleasuring me into pain. He is not using any instrument of pain to get what he wants. Instead of nipple clamps or ball stretchers, he is using soft touches, feathers, fur, leather, latex and his prostate massager to tease me into self torture. I think to myself that this is grossly unfair, and then I remind myself of the collar, jock strap and leg chains I have worn almost constantly since I first stepped into his house.

Even these deviations of thought are not enough to keep my mind and crotch away from the concerted efforts of Master, whom I can hear laughing low in the pleasure he is tormenting me with. He is ball whipping me and pulling on my tit. The stimulation from the balls and vibrator overwhelm me. There is no way I can restrain my cock from overriding my focus, and the ensuing hard on elicits another howl of pain. Master grins and continues, my pain is one I can not drive out. My will as a slave is being pushed to its limits. But Master is too devious to allow me the privilege of release, so he switches to another course of action. His rubber palms begin slapping my chest with just enough force to diminish my erection, and my screams subside into deep moans. His hands pause after I cease to scream. He picks up a feather in each hand and begins softly drawing them across every exposed space of my body. I am fighting so much that I can feel the ropes dig in my elbows and knees, but Master continues his cruel sensual stimulations. I am successful at keeping my cock from stiffness.

That is when Master decides on a change in tactics. No longer satisfied with the mere sight of me squirming on his bed, he begins flicking the feathers between the rings surrounding my cock. This time there isn't even a moment of resistance and my cock springs to life. This time the blood engorged swell is greater than anything prior. No matter how hard I fight my instinctual reaction, it is of no use. My cock gets both ends of Master's acts. It is the direct source of the pleasuring and the recipient of the pain. I can feel the warm twitch in my balls. Master must have incredible instincts for his slaves, because he pulls the feathers away from my cock before I trip into release.

This is as helpless as I have ever been with any Top or Master. The combined orders that he has given me conflict with each other, even as his actions draw me ever closer to compliance or disobedience. If I come, will I be punished for not holding out, or will I be rewarded for obeying Master's request for my slave load? Even the vibrator and its constant reminding stimuli can't keep me from wondering what Master's true desire here is.

And still, Master continues his onslaught. Ball point pens to my feet. Tiger balm on my nipples. Strokes and slaps in any manner of combinations. all reinforced by the rise and fall of a pain filled erection and the accompanying wails of pain and (this far into our day) frustration. Master has barely uttered a word during today's lesson other than chuckle to a satisfactory cry, or "Nice" when he makes me perform a significant jerk in my bonds.

That changes again. Master begins to push something into the outer ring on the gates. I am unable to see what the object is, but when a loud whir emanates from my crotch I know and feel it. He has lodged another vibrator inside the end of the constraining rings and the shiver travels the length of the trap. The vibrator in my ass is now reinforced by the second one on the other side of my body. Master begins to bark orders at me, demanding that his slave produce a load for him. I want to release so bad, but the pain to my cock has stopped me each time, along with Master's regulating the stimulations.

This time there is no escape. There is a burning heat in my nipples, a constant, never ending day long teasing of my prostate, and the complete stimulations of all Master's talents. My erection shoots forward once again into the pain zone, but once it expands fully, the cock head slipping right into the cup of Master's vibrating trap. The tickling tease is too much and the erection holds. I am screaming in horrible agony, even as what is usually an orgasmic feeling of pre-cum begins to flow and drips out from the vibrators cup. Master takes one more advantageous action, as he again slips his gloved hands against my balls.

It is all too much, and even as I scream like I am in a real Hell instead the chastity device christened with the location. My body begins to spasm against the ropes, and I can hear Master prodding me on, even if I am too far gone to understand what he is saying. I am wrenching against my restraints like I am being electrified from head to toe. Suddenly a scream I recognize as mine bursts through the gag, a scream of release. The cup that has imprisoned my cock head is overflowing with stream after stream of slave cum, as Master ordered. The stimulations have been so extended, though, that the ejaculation refuses to stop. It also means that the torture of the gates returns quickly after the initial ecstatic rush. I begin to gag in pain, as my cum continues to fly. There are stars behind my eyes for Master once again, for how long I am not sure. I finally regain control of my senses as the erection finally runs its course. The gates can no longer crush my cock as it retreats away from the torturing rings.

Master has also obtained another of his favorite expressions. After screaming in pain for so long, all I can do after the relatively long ejaculation and the extremely long torture is break into tears from the emotional torpedoing Master has put me through on his bed. Master reaches to the hood, and pulls the gag away. "Very good, slave. Six hours of resistance is very good. I am impressed, slave. I will untie you from the bed, where you can sleep tonight, in my arms. I will awake you for dinner. Now say what all good slaves know, boy."

Weakly, I mumble in a haze of emotions, "Thank you, Master." If Master did awake me for dinner, I do not remember. I do not recall anything until we awoke the following morning, with my ankle chain and collar locked in the position they were on the night Master first brought me into his bedroom, with one addition. There is now a lock tightly pinning my genitals instead of the rubber jock.

"You have one more test, slave. Go out to the garden and use these clippers to obtain one flower. Bring it to me in the manner you see most fitting and be prepared to explain your choice." Master hands me the tool and escorts me, naked and chained, out his back door. His garden is extravagant and well stocked with blossoms of many varieties of plants, and I commence my difficult search.

Once I have reach my decision, I return to Master's door and stand at attention, head bowed. He opens the door to find me with a white rose clenched between my teeth in a submissive stance. He looks at me and then allows me entrance with no comments. I enter his kitchen and again commit to stance. Master stares. After a few more minutes, he accepts the white rose and orders my explanation for the choice.

"Master has instilled many new things to slave this week, Sir. I wanted to give you a rose, because it is the most devious of plants, offering both beauty and blood. It has an intoxicating presence in its scent, as does a Master's intoxicating presence during his training. Too much of a tight grip will draw blood, which Master drew from me. I chose white as the color, because it represents the purest of colors, and of spirit. Master has a true spirit in that he pushed me into spaces I barely believed I could last through, yet nurtured me enough to explode in beauty." I nod my head pensively and await Master's reply.

I am astounded when I hear the crack of emotion in his voice. "Slave," he said softly, "you have given me everything a Master could ask for in the past four days. Obedience of orders, submission, and willingness. But above all else, trust. The most valuable thing a Master can ask for, yet not demand." I see the water welling up in his eyes as he struggles to maintain his composure. he pauses for a minute to bring himself up, and tells me "The envelope I put in the mail is going to your address. My Master/slave contract is in it, as well as a key. The key will unlock the padlock around your cock and balls. When you get home, I expect both the lock and key to be returned. And if you see fit, a signed contract that will grant your entry into my family. Understood slave?"

Now it was my turn to be overwhelmed. "You really wish for me here, Master?"

"Yes, slave I do. I knew from the second day that you were ready, but I always give my prospects the time to go home and ponder the decision. Now get down on your knees and show your respect." I fall to the floor and kiss Master's feet in joy. He pulls me up and unlocks the collar and ankle chains, and tells me to get dressed. He has already laid my plane tickets on the table. I expect my next fare to be one way!

SIGNATURE EDITION

He looked up at me with a smile as I approached the folding table. The bar had set up a spot in the corner for men to come up and buy his latest book There were already a handful of men that had asked him for his signature, and I was there to get one of my own. This was his third book, but the first time he'd come to town for a signing. I'd bought the other two, which fueled more than a few evenings with hard-handed reading. His stories had also led me to try a few things on willing boys in my care. Those words definitely enhanced my kinky sex life along with my time in the playroom, and I wanted to tell him so.

I'd deliberately worn my leather jodhpurs and uniform shirt, since it was one of the stories in his first book that helped me realize a long time rogue police scene. I'd had them made special for that session and it was worth every cent. Being a big man has made it tough to get leather that fits correctly. I'm not a bear, but I'm not a shrimp. Before I'd left San Diego, I'd been recruited to play pro football and spent a couple years in training. Even though the call-up never came, I was still in good enough shape to hold my own. I am also pretty good at turning on the charm when I need to. That made it real nice when he smiled at me. Not as much a smile as a grin, really. The kind of grin that gets me hard, because I want to take that angelic face and see it scrunch up in sweet delicious pain on my table.

"I have both of your books, and I love them. I'm looking forward to reading this one, boy." I handed him a twenty and he gave me a five.

"Why thank you Sir," he replied, his smile still beaming. "Any particular favorite?"

He opened the book to the front page and picked up his marker. "Oh yeah," I replied. "The cop who takes the kid into the warehouse and tricks him into thinking he's a suspect in a cop killing. Got this uniform just to act that one out on my own."

If possible, his smile got broader. "Wow. That's one of the meanest stories I've ever written. That's a real compliment Sir." I think he even started to blush a little. "And if I may add, you look damn good in that uniform Sir."

He signed the page "To the hottest cop in the bar..."

A few more customers came up to the table, and I couldn't monopolize his time. I picked up my copy, thanked him and moved off to the bar. But I kept my eye on him. A slow but steady stream of men came up to him and offered their congratulations, but I never heard him say anything to them like he did to me. After a couple of hours, it seemed as if everyone who wanted a copy had made their purchase, so he put the books that were left behind the bar and sat down on the stool a couple seats down from me. Some of the patrons gathered around him and started to ask him questions about his stories and how he thought them out. He was cordial and took their questions. I had a few of my own, but I just sat back and listened. Some, he said, were from experiences he had, and others from what others had told him about. He mentioned one from his friend Butch God, and another about a whipping scene he'd witnessed as the bottom went into an out-of-body experience. He also talked about other things, like his love of animals and movies, and other friends whose books he admired. He was looking happy with his evening's work, even buying a pitcher of beer for the men who were talking with him. Curiously, I noted, he was the only one in the group that wasn't drinking.

Meanwhile, I started to wonder. What it would take to get him to write about me?

It was beginning to wind down, and I had to step outside for a minute. Ever since the smoking ban took effect, I've been doing that pretty often. I was standing by the back of my Chevy Blazer when I saw him come out, box of books in his hand. That was about when inspiration hit me. I dropped the tailgate of the Blazer and took out a spray can of ignition fluid, and sprayed it on my black hanky. When he had put the box into the car he was using,

I called out to him. He looked over, and smiled again. This smile was a slightly tired smile; I guess the evening had worn him down a little. But he was still nice enough to walk over to me and where I was sitting on the tail gate.

"Hello again Officer," he offered politely. "Thanks for buying my books. I really appreciate the support."

I held the hanky in my gloved hand. "Would you be willing to personalize the others for me, boy?"

"How would you like me to sign them? Do you have them here?" He looked at the metal I was sitting on, but no books.

"No, boy, they're at the house." He took up the space next to me, and sat down as well. It was just what I was hoping for. "I got a hot surprise for you, boy," I told him. Unclenching my gloved fist, I pushed the damp cloth over his face while holding my other hand against the back of his head. He struggled, fought for a few seconds, but I still have more muscle than most. Between strength and surprise, he was soon limp in my arms.

This kind of knockout only has a five-minute window, so I quickly pulled a sack over his head, tied his ankles and cuffed his wrists. He rolled into the back of the Blazer and I flipped the tailgate up. My house was far enough away that he'd come to by the time we'd get there, but I was ready to dose him again. He was kicking up a good racket when I brought the garage door down. I left him in the SUV to prepare my space, delighting in his shouts.

Once I had the dungeon in order, I took the time to get a clean cloth and soak it in genuine ether. It was safer and would give me a longer window of opportunity to get him in the position I needed. He was still struggling and yelling when I opened the back of the Blazer and shoved my gloved hand under the sack over his head. I pressed the cloth against his face till he again went still, and then hoisted his limp body over my shoulder and into the dungeon.

I draped him over my medical examination table, lying face up. Taking the cuffs off, I began to strip him. Slipping his vest off was easy, as was pulling his t-shirt over his head. I fastened my leather restraints to each wrist, and then locked them down to the handles of each side of the table. I coupled the belts that crossed his chest and pulled them firm, watching as his body sank into the table's padding. Then to his pants, first came the belt. I jerked his boots off as quickly as I could unlace them, then pulled his jeans away from his body. I decided to leave his jockeys, and began to secure the restraints to his ankles as he began coming around. He groaned softly as I locked one ankle to the side of the table, but he was aware enough to try and kick as I pulled his second leg down towards the corner. I had to put my full weight on his leg before I could finish locking him down. He gave a pretty good fight over his one free foot, but he was already secured on three points and still a little woozy from being ko'd twice.

"Fuck, man, let me up!" he muttered in protest. After the last thirty minutes of my subduing him, the best he could do was mutter, and that was good. I looked at my guest, all tight and pressed into the exam table's cushioning, his arms locked down at his sides and his feeble protests attesting to his helplessness.

I poured myself bourbon and opened the cabinet next to the man I had just brought home from the bar. I'd been saving a special Maduro for just such an occasion, and gave it a brief dip into the bourbon. Taking a seat across from the exam table, I savored the sight and sound of my favorite writer helpless, confused and more than a little scared. Picking up the book I'd bought earlier in the evening, I idly flipped through the pages. I thought of what I'd overheard him telling the other patrons at the bar about his story ideas before he'd packed up for the night.

"Some." he had said, "are based on experiences I've had, and others from that scenes other men tell me about."

I stared at him for another couple of seconds. The book went back to the cabinet and I took another sip from the bourbon. Then I got up and moved to the table, hovering above him. I let my leathery fingers grip around his cock, still in the under shorts. Giving it a strong squeeze, I brought him to a low moan.

"Remember me, boy?" Another firm squeeze. "You signed your book to 'The Hottest Cop in the Bar.' I decided I'd use that as an invitation to bring you home for the night."

He looked up with me, fear in his eyes. "Please Sir, just tell me what you want."

I smiled at his struggle and his genuine terror. I wanted him to surrender, but I didn't want him afraid of me. Scared about what I might do, yes, but not about the man doing it. I bent over him, my unbuttoned uniform shirt brushing his bare chest. "Right now, the only thing I want from you is submission. I'm sure we've both read 'Misery,' and this isn't it. Just relax, boy, and do as Daddy tells you." I let go of his shorts and, gripping his head in both hands, forced my tongue into his mouth. I jammed it deep, letting it tickle the roof of his mouth and lick against the back of his throat. His resistance was still strong, making his thrashing through my deep kiss all the hotter. He grunted and tried to cry out, but no sound was getting past my mouth or his.

As I let go if his head, he sputtered, "What do you want?"

I picked up the book again and waved it at him. "Exactly what I told you in parking lot, boy. I want to get you to personalize your other books. I just have something in mind other than a magic marker. And something else, but we'll get to that once I get the first part out of the way" I opened one of the drawers in the medical table and produced a leather plug gag. It didn't take much to force it into his mouth, and I buckled it secure. He offered up some fresh protests, but the leather in his mouth effectively stifled those. I took another piece of cord and looped it high on his balls, then began spiraling it down till his twin nuts were forced as low as they could go. "We're going to spend a few hours getting these babies juiced up good, boy," I informed him, slapping my glove against them. "The trick is that you aren't allowed to cum till I'm good and ready for you." I kept tapping his nuts, listening to the moans from behind the gag, ebbing and rising to my rhythm.

A Boner Book

The locks began to clink where they held my restraints down, and the leather padding made creaking noises. I was planning to make this go on for a while, so I couldn't let him think he was going to get off...literally...too easy. Taking the trailing length of the cord down past the edge of the table, I tightened it to an eyebolt that was screwed in just below the lip. It stretched his nuts out, exposing them handsomely to my delights. I want back to the cabinet for my bourbon and cigar, took a little swallow and savor of the drink before making a very deliberate show of clipping the end of the Maduro and lighting it. Blowing the first plumes of smoke across his gag, I reached back down to his nuts and began using the gloves to squeeze them hard, again. His moans turned to grunts and harder "hrrpphhs" as the force of the squeezing increased, along with the blowing of the smoke across his face.

Having read enough of his stories, I figured this would get a rise out of him. He didn't let me down. His dick got harder and gave me a beautiful arch as it lifted from his pubic hair and out from under his shorts. "That's very nice boy," I said, as fatherly as I could, to him. "We need to do away with some of the hair on those balls of yours, though."

I moved the cigar down to his tied off nuts. The soft hiss of singed hair rose from between his lags, and a burst of grunts came from the boy's face. "Don't worry boy. You're in good hands. We just have to stoke up the juice makers with a little heat." He still tried to pull himself back, but the rope that I'd fastened to the end of the table made sure there wasn't much margin for motion. I alternated between heating his balls and cock head to tapping the ashes on his nipples. He was getting more vocal as the cigar got shorter...after all I wasn't going to let a smoke this special get used up entirely without getting a taste of some of it.

At one point during this opening torment, his dick began to droop. Just a little mind you, but noticeable. I let one thumb linger on his tit, but moved the hot end of the cigar under his shaft. The heat rising up towards the exposed cock-flesh had an immediate effect, as he started to struggle hard. "Don't let it fall down boy," I warned him. "You don't want that shaft to fall on Daddy's cigar, do you?" You could see his cock bobble in his panic. He was in no danger of going soft on me, but I chuckled inside as he desperately tried to pump whatever blood he could spare into his hard-on. I pulled the tip away quickly and just watched the pulsing shaft do it's little hot-dance. Unfortunately I had just about finished my treat, and wanted to make sure the boy knew just how special it tasted. I got off my stool and stood back over his gagged head, smiling at him.

"Before I put this out, I want you to sample it yourself. But I really can't take your gag out right now. You'll just have to take it out of me, boy." I took a deep intake of smoke from what was left and held it in my mouth. Then, clamping my lips over his nose, exhaled with equal gusto. The smoke forced it's way down my guest's throat and into his lungs. I held my goatee across his nose like a seal, making sure he had plenty of time to experience the flavor in his gagged mouth and the scent in his trapped nostrils. When I pulled away, the smoke gushed thick from his face and he shook with coughs. I allowed him the time to back catch his breath, and to savor for myself the sight of my guest, more aware than ever of his helplessness and my control.

Once he started breathing normal again, I opened the cabinet and pulled out one of my favorite stimulators. It's a long flesh colored anal probe, with a bulbed tip. It's great for getting a tight prostate to relax and load up some boy juice, and once that rubber bulb starts massage the inner bulb, you just can't fight it. I took my gloves off in order to wave it snakelike over my guest's face and described, in as even tones as I could, my next intent. "This is like the cruelest finger fuck you've ever had, boy," I intoned, letting the bulb caress his neck. Once I get it in you, your cum is just going to start simmering and boiling, and those tied up balls of yours are going to start feeling the juices trickling in. I'm going to get you so full, they'll swell and turn colors for me boy. You're going to beg to cum, but that's not going to happen till you're full like I want you." His eyes rolled back and forth, like the probe was hypnotizing him.

First those shorts were going to have to go. I'd already twisted them around where his nuts were tied off, and they were pulled aside from where I was teasing his cock with the cigar. But they were definably still in the way of his ass. I got a set of shears out and snip-snipped them in his face, just to watch his expression. Letting the cold edge of the blade slip under the waistband, I gave it a hard SNIP and sliced the elastic. The shorts went loose as I cut through to the leg holes and ripped them away. My target now exposed, the shears went back to the table. I tore open a condom and rolled it down the length of the latex shaft, and then squirted a pump shot or two of lube over it. Pumping another glob on my fingers, I began to massage his asshole. His struggles increased as I expected, but I just chuckled and let one finger wriggle inside. The rope to his balls prevented him from pulling up and away as I forced the second finger alongside the first. He was a tighter hole than I would have thought, given all the fucking he's written about.

I used my fingers to get a good approximation of where his little ball was, and then removed my hands from his ass. Before he could relax from that moment, I popped the probe inside and gave it a fast shove into his guts. A surprised YMPPHH! blurted from the gag as I began to slide the probe back and forth, knowing that his prostate was bringing forth more juice each time the little rubber bulb nudged against it. The grunts turned to moans as his resistance gave way to pleasure. I liked knowing that his balls were beginning to load up for me, but it was far too early for me to let him forget his place. I let go of the probe, allowing it to hang half in and half out of his ass. Wiping my hands clean of the lube, I pulled my gloves back on, and then gave his balls a hard strike.

The moan turned back into a howl and his face contorted with confused fear and pain. "What's the matter boy?" I growled at him? "Never been punched?" I gave him two hard fast ones in the ribs to knock the breath out of him. The result was hot...his dick shriveled like an accordion with the air let out. "You remember what you wrote in '9/10ths of The Law' boy? 'Tears are so much more satisfying than screams'? I've always taken that to heart boy. It sums up a lot of why I like to play the way I do." I watched him gasping and heaving, and then I felt something new stir.

"I had a couple drinks at the bar tonight boy, and some bourbon when I brought you in. And you know something? I got to take one fierce piss. Where do you think it should go boy? Hmm?" I loosened my uniform pants and cupped my jockstrap in my gloved hands. "Look what you've done to the Officer, boy. You not only made him hard, but also got his bladder all worked up. Taking a piss with a hard is a pain in the ass boy. If you weren't gagged, you'd be drinking this yourself." I took a seat and removed my boots, then my leather uniform pants. I have a small step stool that I use in the playroom for this kind of occasion, but there's usually a funnel in the mouth of the prisoner. Not that he needed to know this.

Pulling the stool along side the exam table, I stepped up and shoved the mesh of the jock in the face of my guest. Daddy's got one steaming yellow blast he wants to give you boy. I think you'd look good wearing my piss. But that's for another scene, don't you think? I forced my crotch over his nose, cutting off his air for a few seconds, waiting for the protests to start when he needed the air. When I straightened up, I stepped back and went to the cabinet for one of my special toys. Bringing it back to the exam table, I showed the boy my brass bedpan, bought on an online auction. I made him watch as I pissed hard through my jock, the liquid running hot into the pan and catching it. Once I had let it all out, I slid the soaking jock down my legs and held it up, still dripping.

I gave it a quick wringing into the bedpan and got some of the excess piss out of the mesh. Then I held it over the boy's head to let a few drops land on his face. "It's your turn to wear this boy," I informed him. I yanked it over his head and pulled the cup so it rested across his nose, so every breath for the rest of his scene was going to be filled with the intensity of my scent. He threw his head from side to side, trying to shake the cup away, but there was no escaping the heavy soaked cloth across his face. Better than ether, I thought. Not bad for impromptu.

"Now boy," I told him with a grin, "time to get those squirt cannons back to loading." Giving the probe a few slow strokes, I watch him shudder as the bulb gave his prostate a few more tantalizing rubs. "And the best way to get them eggs juicing is to heat them up. Let's get them cleaned off, shall we?" From the cabinet of tools, I got out my razors and a can of shaving cream, and set to work on his pubic hair. The cigar had already singed a few of them away, but I wanted him cleaner. I splashed some water on his crotch and them sprayed the cream thick on his waist. The cold menthol made the goose bumps come up and his shriveled cock twitch, but I took a razor to the area above his cock and scraped a path clear. He obviously wasn't ready for this, and he squirmed under the 'scrrtchh' sound of his pubes coming away. I just chuckled and made another stroke. Then along the side of his shaft, and all around the inside of his legs.

Scrrtch, scrrtch. I let the razor jiggle against the handle of the probe, giving him another uncomfortable reminder of his ass, and stroked away at the lather surrounding the rope on his balls. He was now delightfully hairless around the area I needed to get to, and used a towel to roughly wipe away any remaining cream. I decided there wasn't much I could to his tits after I got the candles out, so I took a pair of butterfly clamps out of the drawer and fastened them to his nipples. His eyes closed as the grips took purchase, and I gave them a good pull to pinch hard. He was getting some blood back in his cock, the jerk on his tits made his cock stir again. I kept jiggling the chain with one hand while sliding the probe around his ass with the other. Within minutes, my guest was back to where I wanted, hard and helpless.

The candles were big and thick, the kind that will collect wax in a big pool so you can either drip it slowly or pour it on thick. His eyes peered around the cup of the jock, as I use my lighter to get the candles started. Silently, I watch as the wax begins to gather in the tops of each candle, and hold them over his chest. I let a tiny drop fall on the center, between his nipples. He gasps, air sucking the piss covered mesh of the jock down into his nostrils. That was an unexpected and delightful side effect. I let the candles drip on each arm, giving the boy the chance to work his way up to the next level. The wax continues to trickle from the angled candles, tiny drops landing on his arms and legs. Each splat is greeted with a moan or gasp, his cock hard and twitching. I stop long enough that he looked up at me, pleading for both the session to stop and for me to go on, and I know it is time to work on him harder.

I decide that speaking softly will make this more intense, so I set the candles down and lean over my guest. I let my tongue dart in his ear, and take the time to nibble his lobes as I jiggle the chain of the nipple clamps. He gives a groan, as his sub-mind is more in play after the sensuality of the early waxing. "We need to hurt you more, boy." I whisper. "Remember what I said about heating your eggs up to get the best juice? Daddy's going to take you there now, Daddy's going to torture you harder than probably anyone before. You're going to scream for Daddy and Daddy is going to get hard hearing you scream. Daddy is going to like seeing you trying to escape. Daddy wants you to know that he kidnapped you to torture the living fuck out of you, for giving him all those beautiful ideas in your books. This Officer is so hot to see you crying in pain that I'm all but naked and I sincerely want to rape that face of yours when we're done with the candles....do you understand, boy?" From his place of helplessness, I hear him sigh; it's the hush of surrender. Inside, I swell with joy.

In addition to the thick candles, I light two long narrow ones. There is already a splattering of wax along his limbs and a few on other parts, but now it's time to get serious. I hold each of the long candles above opposite nipples, and the wax begins to drop. The shining metal of the clamps take the first drops, and his sensitively compressed nipples are awakened as if by electricity. His body arcs with the waves of pleasure pain as each fresh drop adds an extra minute coat to his tortured nipples. Soon the little pile of wax around the clamps has become thick enough that the pain is a numbing, expanding warmth, and I move the trail of wax incrementally lower along his chest. His moans are rhythmic with his breathing and the boy's instinctive knowledge of where this trail of pain is leading. When I cross the edge of his ribs and on to his belly, his whimpers are animal like in their mix of desire and desperation, and his bobbing cock begins to pearl with a first dab of pre-cum.

This slow torment all but freezes time, and the candles continue their insidious path towards the boy's balls. His struggles make the locks on his restraints clink in time to the drops, and jock puffs in and out, each sweet piss smelling inhale a reminder of his captor's power over him. I am at the line where I'd shaved his hairs away, and the sensitivity is much higher. It would take just a mere twitch to allow the first drops of wax to land on his cock head, shaft, or tied off balls. Instead, I allow the drops to linger at the edge of his pubic line, waiting for the boy to look up at me. It takes a few more drops for him to catch on that the motion of the wax trail has stopped, and he opens his eyes and looks at me. I use that second to shift the flame of the candle to the space between his legs, letting the flame flicker ever so briefly across his balls.

He's so surprised that he doesn't even have time to scream. His eyes go wide and his balls jerk in their ropes, I would bet he thinks me insane at this second. I make another pass under his balls, and this time there is a scream, a huge horrified cry that even an outsider would recognize as terror. I cross to the end of the table and flick each candle under the soles of his feet, delighting as he tried like hell to get them away from the licking flames.

I pulled the candles away, blew them out and moved back up the table. "Your Officer said he was going to make you scream, right boy?" Through his cries and thrashing, he still managed to nod yes. I picked up the still burning, thick, candles that I'd set to the side when I'd lit the narrow ones, and held them high over my prisoner's waist. "Then scream now, boy!"

The pooled up wax from nearly a half hour poured down and splashed over the boy's shaft and tied up nuts. I expected this to be his limit and I was not disappointed. He jerked so hard I thought he'd rip the exam table out from the floor of the dungeon, as the spoonfuls of white wax spattered in a final assault on his already supersensitive shaved and worked over, beaten balls and cock. His scream was a toneless wail and his eyes rolled back into his head. Had this been any other session, this would have been a brilliant finale. I'd have brought him off and that would have been the end of it. But not this boy. I had kidnapped him special and there was still one more twisted step I needed to lead him through.

I gave his balls a look; they were starting to get very red. Being so tightly wrapped, waxed, and stretched, they'd been gathering a full reservoir of the juice I needed. "It's about time we opened the pipeline. What do you think, boy?" I undid the knot from under the edge of the exam table, and loosened the top end at the first coil of his balls. Then, with a solid yank, I pulled the rope away like a yo-yo string and watched as his balls whipped round and round in a windmill when the cord spiraled off. The scream this time couldn't hide behind the gag and my prisoner arched, again, to the limits of his restraints. He shook so hard that loose wax flew from his body and balls, landing on the floor next to the table. Tears welled in his eyes and his hard-on slipped down a fraction from the torturous agony of the ball pain.

That was when my resistance broke and I decided to give myself an extra treat. Pulling up the stepstool I'd used when I threatened him with my piss shower, I stood myself over his head and began stroking myself with gusto. My balls were probably as well loaded as his were by now, and the sight of him, pained face crying noiselessly and reeking of my piss-covered jock, was almost enough to drive me home. I needed just a little more, so I grabbed the chain to the tit clamps and pulled them hard. His screams began afresh as I snarled, "Ride it boy! Ride it!" I gave the clamps a jerk so hard they popped off and his screams became operatic. That was what I craved, and, with a gusty bellow, I shot my load into his face, feeling wave after wave rip out of me. My eyes squeezed closed as I dropped the tit-clamp chain and held my crotch in both hands, letting my leather fingers milk the balls dry.

After a few more seconds, I opened my eyes and stepped back to get a look at the results. I had to catch my breath after that. He looked delicious, the gag still strapped tight across his head, the piss soaked jock stretched out over his nose, and my cum running down his forehead and cheeks. As much as his sweaty, smelly submission had propelled me to shoot with lust into his watching face, that really wasn't my original intention. When I grabbed him in the parking lot, I had two goals in mind. It was time to take care of the first. I took a cum-rag from another drawer in the medical table and wiped my cock off, then began using it to crack the wax off his stomach. I needed a clean space for my final act. Once I had his belly and chest wax and sweat free, I took another towel and draped it across my guest's waist, and tickled his semi-erect cock back to full steel over-top of the towel.

I took the book I'd purchased earlier at the bar and laid it, open and pages down, across this stomach area and began massaging his balls with my glove again. He was already hotter than he could almost stand. It wouldn't take much to set him off, and I could feel the scrotum tighten as I tugged on his nuts. His grunts were getting louder behind the gag, and I paused to see the squirming resume. Letting go of his balls so he'd focus back on the man who had him under control, I let him in on the reasons for tonight's session.

"I'm glad you signed my book tonight, boy. But I wanted something a bit more personal than what you gave to all those other men at the bar. I'm sure there are a lot of men who have one of your books that you've written your name in." I took a little squirt of lube and started back to work. Ever so teasingly slow, on his shaft. "In 200 years, though, I want people to be able to say, with one-hundred percent certainty, that you had not only signed my book for me, but that we'd played together." I took my free hand and began to slither the probe in and out of his ass again, and I began to stroke his cock a little faster, watching as his arching and squirming made my cum drip and roll off his gagged face. I had him on the brink...he wasn't going to be able to hold it in much longer. A couple more strokes...

"I want anyone who picks up this book in the future to be able to say that this was you...give it to me boy! Now!!!"

Almost three hours of constant stimulation and torture play had the desired result. From behind the gag came loud delirious groans and his cum sprayed all the way up to his chin. His pulsing cock spasmed again and again, throwing a massive load across his body and all over the front and back cover of the book, just like I'd imagined it would.

"Someday, if anyone wants proof, I'll have it right here. A perfect DNA match from your semen, boy." I lifted the book from his body and set it back on the cabinet next to my chair. I took a drop or two off his chest and smeared it across the title page for good measure. My visitor was breathing hard, his chest pumping under the restraining belts, his juices running off to the side as I pulled the anal probe away from his hole. My juice was still clinging to his face and the jock strap as I began to undo the gag buckle and the locks. He was still far too spent to move as I removed his ankle cuffs and the towel I'd placed across his stomach. I pulled the jock away and plucked the gag from his mouth, and offered his some water. He took it from me with thanks.

Finally free of the gag, he was able to speak. "Is that all you wanted Sir? To play with me because you liked my books?" It was easy to see that this was incredulous to him, something short of a star fuck. Well maybe it was, but I had something a little loftier in mind.

I brought out a red sharpie marker and the first two books for him to autograph for me. "My dear boy, think of me as a key to that perverted muse of yours. Before you go home tonight, I fully expect you to answer 'yes Officer" to my next question. I heard you in the bar, telling people that you wrote some of your best works based on real sessions. I fully expect, no actually, I order you turn tonight's episode into a story for the next collection. You might want to make it a little juicier that what we actually did; I'm sure that imagination of yours can go that far. Just remember that there was a very hot cop who wanted a little something extra to his signature edition of your latest book. What do you say, boy?" Before he could answer, I grabbed his head in my gloved hands just like at the start, when I first had him secured to my table, and forced my tongue down his throat.

This time he didn't resist.

A BRIEF EXPLANATION

I had to make a decision regarding whether or not to include this next piece in "Sgt. Vlengles' Revenge" for a couple of reasons. The first, and most obvious, being that it really isn't a fiction sex piece. The other in the fact that it's a humor piece that, upon its original publication, really pissed a lot of people off! So perhaps a brief explanation is in order. "There's No Such Thing as a Pushy Bottom" evolved out of two places. The first was a stand up comedy routine I'd done about pets ruining lovemaking sessions. The other was my kidding a friend with the line that Tops are mostly men with time management issues. I did a few of these jokes at an Avatar presentation in Los Angeles got enough laughs to write about a few more thoughts on the subject. Mitch at Sandmutopian Guardian knew a good muck stirrer when he saw one and asked if he could run the piece as a satire and I was more than happy to agree. The response was, to say the least, outspoken. I'd underestimated that the best leather jackets are carved from the sacred cow, and Mitch received an above average amount of mail concern my audacity. Etc. Oddly enough, this particular article has since taken on a life of its own. I've seen it on a few websites (with only one giving me a writer's credit) and a handful of clubs used it on their newsletters. The response is still the same in that some get it and the rest think I am wronger than wrong for daring to make the suggestions. Then again, if I have managed to write something that manages to provoke the snittiest fits of red faced sputtering, then perhaps "There's No Such Things as a Pushy Bottom" really does belong in a book that carries the subtitle "and other abuses of power."

Enjoy.

THERE'S NO SUCH THING AS A PUSHY BOTTOM

(AND OTHER MYTHS DEBUNKED)

Why is it every frigging Master/Top on Planet Earth thinks they know it all...or at least enough to write books? There are all these guidebooks for being the perfect slave/boy/bottom and with few exceptions, all are written by men claiming to be Tops. Wait a second, let's amend that. The proper phrasing should be "frustrated Tops." Because most of these crazed typing dominants never get it right. I'm not just saying this so I can pick up a few extra welts this weekend, either. That's also part of the myth. Slaves don't "need" to be enslaved, baby cats. If that were the case, boatloads of men would be racing up the ramps for spots by the oar chain. So get over that one, too. Any Master who suddenly decides to exercise his hands on a keyboard instead of their anatomy is probably writing his Master/slave credo from a day's worth of sexual boredom rather than anything he did to a boy that day!

So Masters from coast to coast attempt defining what true universal slavery is all about, while slaves wind up getting manifestos of what that particular Master wished he'd get his clutches into that day, month or however long he bemoaned the lack of committed bottoms for him to take to the dungeon.

You know it too, big guy study Master dude. So let this slave lob some cream pies at y'all and turn the tables on some of the far more prevalent myths.

Myth Debunked #1: The Legendary "Pushy Bottom"

If you, good Sir, consider your bottom to be pushy, let's look at it from a different angle. There is no such thing as a "pushy bottom." All Tops Have Time Management Problems. Think about it: Leatherboy is expected to do every menial task in the condo that Master couldn't be bothered with. Master expects slave to finish these tasks inside of a day. At the same time, the stack of newspapers next to Master's workspace has been piling up since about 1959, the milk containers are still the glass variety and the earliest Metro phone book has less than 200 pages. This is a syndrome that should be called by its real name: "Master Overload." The slave's assignments of the day are to do domestic chores, water the garden, clean the car, get the meals, shine the leathers and check the mail, still saying "Yes Sir" and genuflecting at Master's boots at least 15 times before sundown.

In other words, the project order of a 5-man contracting team and a workload that exhausted Master before he got as far as putting a quarter in the newspaper vending machine.

Now while slave is busy getting the grocery list organized, Master decides that slave should draw Master's bath and fetch his prize squeaky tugboat toy; he calls slave a pushy bottom if slave tells Master Sir was expected at such and such an appointment 15 minutes ago and a bath really isn't advisable at this time. Is slave "Pushy?" Nawwww. Said Master just couldn't get off the sofa to wet-nappy himself if slave wasn't there to pull the tear string.

Which Leads to Debunkarie #2: "All slaves Stand in the Shadow of the Master"

A true Master doesn't cast a shadow. A true Master becomes the center of the slave's solar system and therefore emanates nothing but light. It henceforth becomes the slave's eternal duty to make sure no shadows eclipse the face of his Master. That a slave is somehow enshadowed comes from the same mentality to produce the notion demanding all slaves give up self and ego. This silly precept is one made up only recently: frankly, real slaves have names. Any wannabe Master believing previous slave owners of past centuries had the inclination to contort slaves into littering their speech with "SIR! this slave this" or "SIR! this boy that," is dumber than a gunnysack-load of collars. The great Mastermen of history had no time for such brainwashing nonsense: boy Norman was out doing the necessary plantation picking and quarry digging. Master may choose to give his slave a new name or just simply refer to him as "slaveboy," but the first person who put in a "Master/slave manual" that the prospective slave strip himself of any self worth or identity on Day One should step downstage for his proverbial fruit salad shower. Because if a Master thinks slave is standing in Sir's shadow, Sir'd better look around and make sure of the light source.

Myth Debunked #3: "Real Masters Own Pets"

What's the easiest way to stop a hot scene stone cold dead? It ain't the safe word. Just let Fluffy get into the dungeon. You may think you're the meanest, butchest, hard-assed Whipmaster this side of the Alamo. But if the last thing your bottom sees through the slits in his hood before Master and puddin' tat head for the kitchen is "Master" picking up said snack-insistent feline, forget it. Believe me, on the way out Fluffy is giving your dangling slave meat a look that translates to "Master's house, my rules. Get used to it, you insignificant biped." Only the slave and animal know who really wears the chaps in this household. (Other dead giveaway: Master's prize whip has a pink carpet shred on the tip and is used as Fluffy's favorite chase toy.)

Myth Debunked #4: "I'm Top Only"

Talk about your fourth great lie. Any man who says this will likely be caught saying something later, like ". . . and I can hold my own legs up, boy."

Myth Debunked #5: "Perfect slave Body = Perfect Self Discipline"

"You could stand to lose a few pounds." Any attempted master to utter those words in MY presence is usually met with, "And you, good Sir could use some plastic surgery and a fresh bottle of Grecian formula." Why is it that every Top who demands that slave enter a gym workout program and spend at least six hours each week getting another eighth of an inch on that forearm (between folding the linens and dropping off those 25 years worth of bundled up National Geographics at the recycling center, one supposes) looks like the "before" photo of a Jenny Craig ad? Naturally, if slave balks, he is reprimanded for lacking "self discipline." Being Master's 24/7 boy, carrying a full college courseload and a part time job while being at Master's sexual beck and call has nothing to do with "self discipline." Only getting one more pair of abs to pop out of that washboard stomach does.

Myth Debunked #6: Tops Write These Articles

Frankly, most Masters think "command 'p'" should be followed by directions to the 'loo. Which is probably where most of them are reading this article before calling on slaveboy to come daddyfloss Sir's hieny (of course Master will do this while boy is in the kitchen stuffing the manicotti).

And Finally, Myth Debunked #7: Real Masters Don't Need slaves, slaves Need Masters

Only a partial myth. It's true! Many Masters really don't need slaves.

They need Mommies.

— - — - — - — - — - — - — - — - — - — - — - —

Written Note:

I bought myself a new pair of sneakers before I submitted this article, so any attempt at chasing me down had better be well thought out. I welcome comments from all Tops and bottoms. (And to slaves, please make sure your Master knows where the spellchecker command is....) Just repeat after me, it's only a satire, it's only a satire........

HIGH ROLLERS

Las Vegas, Nevada, playground of the Western World, facades and bait. I know it's built with one specific goal: lure people into shiny box-full-of-money-traps that all look exactly the same once you get past the gaudy pyramids, fake movie lions or elaborate Arthurian motifs on the outside. We think we all know the difference between fantasy and reality. Reality is the one that nobody believes in anymore, I'm beginning to think. So much of the last two days spent suspending reality! Gaping at a fantasy world of stages, singing men and dancing girls, vanishing tigers and the constant seduction of easy fortunes and fast winning disguised as entertainment. It helps me explain why I'm walking away from one of the many 21 tables with nothing left in my wallet but the return ticket home.

I hadn't even gotten lucky in any other sense of the word; despite packing some gear and paying a few visits to the Buffalo, my room in the Hotel remained single during my entire week. As much as anyone wants to claim that Las Vegas is a place where anything could happen, so far the only people that it might have happened with were blue hair ladies and retirees in polyester suits who lust only at the spinning wheels of slot machines and the pocket that could dispense their future in a bag full of silver dollars.

Some of these machines go way back. The new machines were just random number generators with bells and whistles; the real hard-core slots had solid iron arms that only a hard mentality gambler or a real man could yank down. Maybe that's why everyone starts looking the same. Gamblers and tourists come and leave but the machines have outlasted even the sturdiest of the addicted. The carpets in front of these machines were worn from the force a man exerts while making his silver dollar generate a potential win. You didn't just win on a machine like this, either. You beat it. You earned the payoff. You forced the machine to give you what you wanted, or they took you for what you came in with. Nothing more or less. I saw men and women in this row of antiques, machines from a past where public relations didn't exist. Tourists weren't invited to gamble in this aisle. Only the true believers and the moneymen of old.

I slipped my hand into my pocket for the room pass card and felt something metal and round. Laughing mirthlessly, I pulled out one last silver dollar that had somehow missed my fingers till this second. Well, I thought to myself, as deep as my abyss could be, my pocket lining couldn't be any shallower. The face on the dollar scowled at me and I looked to the rows of hardened men trying to strong arm the old slots into submission. No use in keeping any souvenirs, I figured, and stepped up next to another oddly familiar man expressionlessly dropping silver into a machine. I saw merely a nod in my direction as I dropped that last silver dollar into "Old Chief" and used all the muscle my right arm contained to pull that handle down. "Bottom's up," I said to no one in particular.

I figured the old metal box would swallow the dollar and I'd use that last piece of rejection to return to my room and sulk until my bus left Monday. Maybe a double cherry to give me $10 for dinner if there was any justice. But as I muttered my little joke, the man next to me turned and winked, allowing me a small glimpse of a rubber T-Shirt under the button down collar. That's when I heard the crunching wheels spin and clank like a real machine, ratcheting gears and pins and as I watched, one silver bar, then another, and a third, all Ching Ching Chinged into place.

The gambler with the rubber collar next to me: "Young man, your luck is about to change."

The blood drained from my face as twenty pieces of silver fell noisily into the machine's winner cup and an alarm bell began ringing above my head. Red and green lights flashed on either side of me and all the hardened gamblers stopped to look for that fraction of an instant. The bars in this one-armed bandit all blared JACKPOT in my face as the floor boss and security man came over to see who the lucky boy was. In just one pull of a cast metal lever, I had been transformed from invisible washout to floor celebrity; my drop off the canyon wall merely a jump into the winners' pantheon. The man in the expensive suit and the uniformed man with the nightstick asked me if I was alright, then led me off to the metal door that hid the palace treasures.

The Suit smiled at me and offered me his congratulations. "Odds on that machine are about 380 million to one," he informed me. "You don't mind if we quick search you?" I was still in such a state of shock that all I could do was nod yes, and they ran a metal detector over my jacket and sleeves to make sure I wasn't carrying magnets or hijacking devices. Another man with a tool belt entered the office and pronounced that the machine was "clean." That made the security guard relax and the executive smile. "Guess what?" he said in his best official hospitality voice. "You just broke the bank. What's your name?"

I think my heart was finally starting to regain its normal rhythm about then. "Martin," I told them, "Martin Deiner." I gave them my driver's license to prove it and my room receipt. They punched the information into a computer and got confirmation that I was just a regular tourist who suddenly set off some fireworks. "I hate to sound ignorant, but how much do I get?"

The executive (his nametag read John something) turned and looked at me. That was "Old Chief" you just won on, son. He pays off maybe once every fifth year, and you just nailed it. That's two million coming your way. One hundred thousand for each silver piece you got. It may cost us tonight but the tourists will be coming to look at him for weeks. Luck draws like ants to honey, son. Hotel check good?"

I lost my speaking skills.

John something just laughed again. "I'll take that as a 'yes' then. Welcome to the Millionaire's Circle, son. Gill, page Mitch, will you?" John something turned his gaze back to me. His ancient smile never faltered for a second as he handed me a hotel check and a contract to sign. "This informs you of your legal duties and taxes you have to take care of as a winner. Once you've been escorted out of the hotel, we aren't responsible for the monies you've won. But just your luck, the man who was playing the machine right next to you is also one of our bank agency men, his name is Mr. Mitchell and he has a credit line here. If you want, his company limo will take you to his office and he can arrange to have the check cashed on the spot or even electronically deposited in your account back in LA." The security buzzer came on again and John something keyed the door locks. In walked the man with the rubber t-shirt just barely showing overtop his white collar.

"Well, well, well," he smiled down. "How's the high roller?" He certainly remembered me, and was one who wouldn't easily be missed. His suit was expertly tailored to fit a body that had gone to some lengths to stay in very good shape. His moustache was neatly trimmed and his skin, eyes and voice contained the same kind of tone that emitted an aura of old money. He must have been from a European family that knew how to take charge of bankrolls and ledgers when the times called for it. In short, this man exuded control. I could feel it in my bones. If anyone else here had taken notice of the rubber shirt, they weren't making it obvious. A strong handshake as he introduced himself as Armand Mitchell. "I understand you may need my services today?"

I was finally beginning to get my sensibility back, and with it, a better sense of my own power in the situation. "I've had a slight change of fortunes...from bum to millionaire in less than a day. Do you get people like me often?" Both John something and Armand liked that one; they laughed.

"Of course not," John replied. "We get people who win a chunk of cash, we escort them in here, pay them and before they leave for dinner, they've played it all at the wheels. You, on the other hand, we couldn't even hope to take it from you today. Tomorrow perhaps?"

John something asked the last question with just enough scary eagerness to make me click back into reality as a belief system. "I don't think so. Mr. Mitchell, if it isn't too late, could we deposit this check so that I don't have to carry a million bucks on the bus?"

"Young Martin, you seem to be missing something. You're a millionaire as of today." His smile broadened enough to let me notice that, for the first time, he seemed genuinely amused. "You won't be taking buses anymore. Come with me, and for now please call me Armand."

Armand had such a natural confidence that following him out of the office didn't need much decision-making. I felt the string of bumpy zeros pressed into the business check the Casino handed me, looked at the "Pay to the order of" red and green lettering lines and let the moment sink in. He led me out to a long blue limo and a man in a uniform opened that door for me. Armand just smiled and stood next to the limo door, waving me in. As he climbed in next to me and I caught yet another glimpse of the rubber shirt, he asked me "So, would you like your congratulatory drink in my office or at the Buffalo?" My head whipped to face him and his smile was broader than ever. "I saw you there last night, desperately trying to hook up with a Top. I was in my leathers at the time and you didn't notice me. But I saw you." I took a hard swallow and said that I was there and apologized for not seeing him. He laughed again. "I make it a habit of watching and knowing what is going on without being noticed. There are too many sugar babies in this town that would try to suck up to me if they knew my job. So Martin...boy...do you like the rubber shirt?"

The question was meant to be answered in no other manner than "Yes Sir."

"Good then. Open my buttons and get a good look at it." The limousine rolled on as I did what I was told. If this body was anywhere near me in the bar, I wish I knew how I'd missed it. But Armand was right. I was trying so hard to get a particular Leather Daddy to pick me up that I wasn't paying much attention to anybody else. I also thought that there would be at least one other person in Las Vegas in rubber, but that night at the bar, it was just me. Now here I was with a two million dollar check next to a Rubberman in the back of a stretch limo, a hot Rubberman with a penchant for giving orders like "Worship my shirt." My tongue was in high gear and life was suddenly getting much better.

The limo pulled up in the rear of a concrete building and into a security double gate. "Drinks in my office, then." Armand's driver opened the door and the full chest and solid abdomen of my host shimmered in the bright illumination of the security area. He led, I followed. The building was the usual opulence of Vegas but the expensiveness was more a reflection of taste as opposed to mere mad spending. The marble was subdued in color and the carpets were plush and dark. Armand led me to an elevator and used a key to indicate the floor. "That way," he said "no one disturbs me in my private offices." When the elevator doors reopened, there was a glorious display in front of me. This was a man's office, husky in colors, powerful in decor. It was better than an LA movie set, it was real.

Armand remotely turned on a computer and sat down behind a massive desk. "I'll need your account number and two identifications." I handed him a driver's license and social security card. "Thank you." Without even looking up, "Take off your clothes." I hesitated. "This office is clothing optional for after hour guests." So much for subtlety. I stripped for Armand. He was still working on the transfer and, without looking at me, told me to go to a red mahogany chest. "Take out what's in there and replace it with what you just took off." Inside the drawer was a pair of black rubber shorts and tank top. Laying my clothes inside, Armand raised himself from behind his throne and took a look at me in my nudity. I clutched the rubber gear.

"Your transaction is complete. There's two million dollars in your account waiting for you. Put on the shirt. Then we'll talk about investments." He removed his jacket and hung it from a coat tree; giving me a look at his elegant chest and the rubber shirt he'd been wearing that evening. Armand looked equal parts scholarly and stern. "Come to the front of my desk." He cast his eyes at me, then ordered "Kneel!" On my knees in the front of this altar to business, Armand came forward. "I took a look at your credit record. Not very impressive. Same for your employment history. Rather spotty, eh? I think you need a little discipline in your economic ventures...for starters."

I kept my head bowed down as the lecture continued. "I've wanted a partner here for quite some time. If you like what you hear so far, stay on your knees." I didn't budge. "Tonight you have more money than you'd ever earn at your job in over 100 years. Judging from your past, you'd likely run through all of it in about two. If you listen to what I have to say, you'll never worry about bus tickets and retail jobs again. What I offer you is very demanding in nature and will take you every day for the rest of your life to master."

A long narrow white cane appeared before my bowed head, reaching to the floor. "If you find this offer agreeable, kiss the rod." My lips pressed against the Master's tool. "My friendships and contacts in these areas are limited deliberately so I can invest an appropriate amount of time in the 'right' friends. I manage to do well by those I care for. It will be worth it, as will be the times we spend together in the future." Beyond belief! All that time as a poor boy sales clerk in LA, looking for a "real" Master, and here I was getting offered the position I'd lusted for all my life. In a very wealthy financial officer's palace, staring down an evil looking cane held just an initiation's swing from servitude. Armand spoke again, "Can you accept the discipline of following my orders?"

"Yes Sir!"

"Then bend over, Young Martin."

I knew what was coming; the slicing of air didn't surprise me at all. My new Master was a man of considerable muscle, you could tell that just by looking at him. It's just that first hit was enough to still make me launch like a frog.

"Boy," growled Armand. "Discipline means holding still for me when I'm giving you your twelve strokes."

"Yes Sir!"

"Because this is your first time under my hand, you will be forgiven the initial transgression."

"Sir, thank you Sir."

Armand looked at me in a bemused manner. "You do have the proper answers and tone down, boy. Now show my cane the respect you know it deserves. Position yourself."

I got back on my knees in front of Armand's desk, still in the rubber shirt, bare ass raised in a prone manner.

Swish! "Two Sir, thank you Sir. May I have another Sir?" Swish! "Three Sir…" and the air kept tearing apart. Stings gave way to searing, red-hot sensations as my gratitude rose along with my voice. "Five Sir, thank you Sir. May I have another Sir?" Sweat burns began to mix with the mind-blowing pain of the strokes as my own body reacted to Armand's power. Swish! "Seven Sir, thank you Sir. May I have another Sir?" Swish! Tears began raging down my face and my voice wasn't anything I controlled. "Eight Sir, thank you Sir. May I have another Sir?" No turning back...Swish! "Nine Sir, thank you Sir. May I have another?" Swish again! ...until my bawling eyes and watered out voice could barely whimper the final "Twelve Sir, thank you Sir!" My ass was on fire! I knew without looking that there would be monster welts and probably bloody, wicked cuts. Some unmistakable boarding school head mastering was included in Armand's old world background! My hands were still against the front of my head, sobbing into the carpet in front of his desk while I tightly clutched the rubber briefs.

"Young Martin, do you still wish to remain under my tutelage?" The long white cane appeared in front of my head again, touching the floor in front of my face. "If you do, kiss the instrument of correction." I could barely see my Master's rod in front of my blurry eyes, but I managed to get my lips on the cane a second time. The smell of my own blood surrounded it. Armand produced a thick black cloth to wipe the cane down in the fashion of a matador cleaning his sword. Long powerful strokes to clear the blood of the bull he had just conquered.

A degree of warm respect entered Armand's voice. "Rise, boy, and put on your briefs." I pulled the rubber pants over my welts. I had to bite my tongue and force down a cry of pain when the cuts' blood and my sweat began to commingle under the pressure of the tight latex. After he lowered himself into a majestic wooden chair against the wall, Armand tossed a cushion to the floor off to his right. "Sit."

Well, I damn sure tried to sit. There was a certain amount of sadistic glee in Armand's eyes as he watched me trying to squirm into a position that was the least uncomfortable. He undid his pants and pulled out a gorgeous uncut cock, already oozing jiz. My focus shifted immediately from the pain across my ass to the thought of that cock in my mouth. Armand started talking at me again.

"From here on, I will control your finances and be giving you a regular allowance in the form of interest payments, otherwise, you will receive no other monies except what your business accounts earn as pertains to my investments. Officially, you are one of my clients. Off the books, you are one of my boys, and you will answer to my calls whenever I need you. You have nothing else to worry about other than orders I give you, and you always wear your rubber when in your Master's presence. Understood?"

Finally, an excuse to leave the anthill that was Los Angeles and serve out my long-buried fantasy of being a sex slave! The answer was simple and quick.

"Yes Sir!"

"Then get over here and suck your Master's cock" I did exactly as ordered...with gusto. My lips wrapped themselves tightly around my Master's other rod, spit-Lubing it quickly and bobbing to beat the teller. The flavor of him expanded in my mouth and his musky ball-scent tingled my nostrils. His hands dug into the rubber shirt he had chosen for me and the smell of it filled our space. Armand was very pleased, and said so in the manner I would learn to expect when he was at his most aroused. "Good boy. Let me explain to you how the money market operates..."

ABOUT THE AUTHOR

Tim Brough was born in May 1960 and grew up in Central Pennsylvania eating Hershey candy and Lebanon Bologna. He became a bookworm and lost all his body hair by the time he was seven-the condition is known as Alopecia. By the seventies, in addition to being the family bookworm, he started discovering he was a rock and roll freak.

Tim discovered that not only did he enjoy writing, he had a genuine flair for it. After graduating from Palmyra High School in 1978, he was off to Susquehanna University where along with his studies he found himself doing stand-up comedy, singing in a punk band and even dressing up as a clown for a summer at Hershey Park.

In 1989, Tim Brough stumbled across his first copy of DRUMMER magazine in San Francisco while attending a Radio Broadcasting convention. Having his mind blown open by the experience, he left the vanilla world of Delaware behind and took a writing/editing job in Los Angeles. It was in SoCal that he began explorimg this part of his psyche further and to pursue a new career as a broadcast journalist. Tim came out full bore as a Gay Leatherman in the pages of the Oct 11 1993 edition of the magazine he edited at the time while living in Nashville TN. When that publication folded in 1994, it was back to LA, where he got a second wind as a writer and editor. His byline has appeared in magazines as varied Radio & Records, Fetish, Leather Journal, Eagle, Cuir, Frontiers,

Bunkhouse, Mach, Powerplay and his own two major publications, the ground breaking Rubber Rebel and Vulcan America. Tim still is the editor and principle writer/photo-grapher for Vulcan-America.com, which has been providing "Rubbermen, Macho Fetish and Fantasy" online since 1999.

Tim has also participated in all sorts of other exploits, including the infamous Rubber Buddha episode of HBO's SEXBYTES series. If you met him during this period, it's likely been at a leather event with the Louisville Nightwings, or at the Chain Drive Bar in Austin Texas, (the city he spent most of 1997 torturing the nation one phone call at a time as a long distance telephone service telemarketer), or at events such as IML, or the Cell Block Chicago's ongoing Mr. International Rubber competitions where he has frequently been invited to act as a judge, as well as the recently founded Mr. East Coast Rubber in NYC. He also appeared as Brutux Kahn in the Zeus/Can-Am production "Brutal Kombat." This is his second book, *Black Gloves White Magic* being his first which was a huge hit in Spring of 2003.

Even though Tim has laid down roots in seven states, he currently calls Philadelphia home. He is currently working on several novels.

THANKS FOR READING!

W O O F !

Finally, A Book About The Care And Training Of The Human Dog! If You Dont Know What That's About, Then This Is A Book Your Definately Going To Have To CHECK OUT!